The hair on Audrey attention.

"Hello?"

Something hard and unyielding came up and over her head and pressed against her throat, cutting off her air supply. Silencing her. The scrubs slipped from her fingers. Reaching up, she gripped the stick. *Can't breathe.*

She couldn't dislodge it. He was immovable, her captor, his arms and chest forming a vise around her.

Dots danced in her vision. She struggled. Writhed. Kicked. Her lungs stretched to the bursting point.

Audrey reached up to claw at his face. If she could gouge his eyes–

He increased the pressure, consciousness ebbed.

Suddenly, shouts pierced the black cloud. The arms around her went slack.

Audrey swayed and fell to her knees. A scuffle ensued between her attacker and would-be rescuer. In the murky light, she recognized the stark white dressing on the second man's arm.

He shouldn't be here. Shouldn't be engaging a murderer in his condition, most likely the same man who tried to kill him mere days ago.

"Julian," Audrey gasped.

Karen Kirst was born and raised in east Tennessee near the Great Smoky Mountains. She's a lifelong lover of books, but it wasn't until after college that she had the grand idea to write one herself. Now she divides her time between being a wife, homeschooling mom and romance writer. Her favorite pastimes are reading, visiting tearooms and watching romantic comedies.

Books by Karen Kirst

Love Inspired Suspense

Explosive Reunion
Intensive Care Crisis

Love Inspired Historical

Smoky Mountain Matches

The Reluctant Outlaw
The Bridal Swap
The Gift of Family
"Smoky Mountain Christmas"
His Mountain Miss
The Husband Hunt
Married by Christmas
From Boss to Bridegroom
The Bachelor's Homecoming
Reclaiming His Past
The Sheriff's Christmas Twins
Wed by Necessity
The Engagement Charade
A Lawman for Christmas

Visit the Author Profile page at Harlequin.com for more titles.

INTENSIVE CARE CRISIS

KAREN KIRST

⬥ HARLEQUIN® LOVE INSPIRED® SUSPENSE

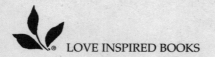 LOVE INSPIRED BOOKS

Recycling programs for this product may not exist in your area.

ISBN-13: 978-1-335-23230-4

Intensive Care Crisis

www.Harlequin.com

Printed in U.S.A.

But as for you, ye thought evil against me;
but God meant it unto good, to bring to pass,
as it is this day, to save much people alive.
—Genesis 50:20

To my dear friend Rebecca Sardella.
Your support and enthusiasm for my stories have been
a great source of encouragement. Thank you.

Acknowledgments

A huge thank-you to Edelyn Bishop, RN, MSN, MBA.
Your medical knowledge and input
during this process were invaluable.

Thank you to my niece, Jessica Felker, RN, BSN.
You were a great source of information,
especially during the planning of this story.

Any mistakes were my own.

ONE

Someone was harming her patients.

Audrey Harris was determined not to let anything happen to the force-recon marine currently in her care. Not only was Sergeant Julian Tan her neighbor, but he was also in her father's unit. Fortunately, the recovery room where she worked had only three patients this morning, and they weren't scheduled to receive more until after lunch.

She reassessed the IV lines and inspected the dressing on his lower arm.

"My team," he murmured, shifting restlessly beneath the thin sheet. "Have to reach them."

Audrey winced. His team was gone, their deaths the result of a training exercise gone horribly wrong. Julian had escaped with several broken bones in his left arm and wrist. The first surgery—performed a month ago, at the time of the accident—had been a success, but he'd had an allergic reaction to the stitches. They'd had to go back in and replace them.

His head lifted from the starched pillowcase. "Where are they?" he demanded in a thick, slurred voice.

"You've had a surgical procedure and will feel groggy for a while. As soon as the anesthesia wears off, I'll take you to post-op." Typically, those nurses would retrieve him, but she wasn't letting him out of her sight.

His eyes, shimmering like copper pennies in a fountain, narrowed in confusion. "I'm in the hospital? Where are the others?"

She'd been on shift when he'd been brought in with the marines who'd initially survived the helicopter crash. While she hadn't been assigned to him, she remembered he'd responded poorly to anesthesia and woke disgruntled.

Audrey wished he didn't have to relive the news of his fellow marines' deaths. Coming around to the other side of the bed, she laid her hand on his shoulder.

"Julian, is the anti-nausea medicine I gave you working?"

He pinched the bridge of his nose.

"Are you feeling sick to your stomach?"

When he didn't answer, she clicked off the overhead light. "Try and rest, okay?"

She started to move away. His uninjured hand clamped over her lower arm, preventing her from leaving.

"Who are you?"

The strength in his grip surprised her. Not because of his physique—he was hewn from steel, it seemed, his body the military's version of a living weapon—but because he was still suffering the effects of powerful medication.

Audrey covered his large, calloused hand with her own, trying to reassure him with her touch. "Audrey Harris. We live in the same apartment complex."

Julian's face remained blank. Even fully alert, she doubted he'd remember her. He wasn't the sort to flirt and make small talk, like some of the single male residents. When he wasn't off saving the world, he went about his daily life with single-minded focus. She passed him sometimes on his way to the apartment's gym and indoor pool.

The squeak of rubber soles on the polished tiles heralded her coworker's arrival. "How's our wounded warrior doing?"

Chasity Bateman's sparse eyebrows lifted at the sight of their joined hands. Audrey separated herself from his hold and pulled aside her friend and fellow nurse.

"He's out of sorts, and who can blame him?"

"Good thing he has a pretty nurse to distract him from his troubles." Stray blond curls peeked out from her surgical cap.

"I don't date patients."

"You don't date *anyone*. That's the problem."

Audrey glanced at the bed. His eyes were closed, his spiky lashes forming dark crescents against gold-dust skin. Julian Tan was a striking man. Short, sleek brown-black hair framed proud, angular features offset by a generous mouth. He was strong and handsome, but intense and private. In their one exchange, when her father had introduced them, she'd gotten the impression that few people were allowed into his personal circle.

"A handsome, intriguing guy like him could be the one to make you finally forget about Seth."

Grief pinched her—less potently than in the past, which troubled her. "I can't forget."

Chasity nudged her. "There's no crime in having a little fun. Seth wouldn't begrudge you that."

"Shouldn't you be with your patients?"

The recovery area in their modest-size hospital consisted of a single, long room with beds lining both walls and an aisle in the middle. There were privacy curtains, but none were currently in use. Near the entry doors, two women occupied beds opposite each other. Both were quiet.

Too quiet?

"What happened last week was a fluke, you know," Chasity said, picking up on her sudden anxiety.

Audrey tugged on the ID card hanging around her neck, then allowed it to snap back into place. "A fluke? Alex Shields had an allergic reaction that could've killed him. Wanda Ferrier came in for outpatient surgery but wound up staying five days because she was given the wrong dosage." Her heart pounded with remembered dread. "Someone stole my log-in, Chasity, and deliberately set out to harm my patients."

Her friend was unable to mask her skepticism. "I know it's hard to accept that we're capable of mistakes, but we all get busy and distracted."

"This isn't a case of simple carelessness. I'm being made to look incompetent."

All because she'd done the right thing. In recent weeks, she'd noticed inconsistencies between the supply list and the actual supplies in their stockroom. More serious was her suspicion that an Onslow General employee was diverting narcotics and other medicines. She'd spoken to a handful of her coworkers in the surgical unit, but they hadn't had useful information to share. So she'd taken her concerns to the charge nurse. Veronica "Iron Nurse" Mills had promised to look into the matter. That was when the mishaps started. Audrey could only conclude that the thief was attempting to discredit her.

The swish of a door interrupted their exchange, and in walked the taskmaster who ruled the department with an iron fist. Veronica was tall for a woman and of an indiscriminate age. Her brassy yellow hair was styled in fat sausage rolls reminiscent of a bygone era. She wore her uniforms starched and was never seen without her trademark fire-engine-red lipstick. Since Audrey's transfer from the ICU to surgery eighteen months ago, she'd gotten the impression that Veronica disliked her more than anyone else. And since she was displeased by most everyone and everything, that was saying something.

Her broad nose pinched at the sight of them. "Heather's gone home with a fever. You'll have to spend the rest of your shift in pre-op, Chasity."

Her friend cast Audrey a sideways glance, then inclined her head. "Of course."

When the petite blonde had gone, Veronica's gray gaze swept over the three occupied beds. "I trust you'll be able to handle yourself?"

The underlying message was clear—no more messups.

"Yes, ma'am."

She sniffed. "See that you do."

The next twenty minutes passed in a blur, as one of the female patients roused and promptly vomited. While Audrey was tending to her, the other woman's vitals started fluctuating, calling for her to investigate the issue. She didn't like that the hospital was understaffed. Typically, in the recovery area, each nurse was assigned to one patient. But HR had been slow in replacing the employees they'd lost. In recent months, two nurses had moved out of the area, one had quit to be a stay-at-home mom and yet another had accepted a different position in the hospital.

"Please, I need water." The girl who'd gotten ill was perspiring.

Audrey looked down the aisle at Julian. Because of his history of responding poorly to anesthesia, Chasity had thought it best to place him apart from the others. He appeared to be resting comfortably.

She wouldn't be gone long. Five minutes, tops. "I'll get you some ice chips."

"Thank you." The patient gave her a weak smile.

In the hallway, an X-ray technician strode past, acknowledging her with a simple nod. David was a new hire. Quiet and introverted. Heather in pre-op had a crush on him. Something about his small, shifty eyes made Audrey think of him as stalker material.

She waited until the hallway was clear before hurrying to the room where they kept sodas and snacks for patients. There were three nurses in line ahead of her. Stifling a sigh, she experienced a rising tide of unease. *It won't happen again. It can't. Not on my watch.*

Julian was on the helicopter again. He felt it list sharply to the right. Saw the ground racing up to meet them. Heard the other guys' warning shouts. Smelled the stench of gasoline and blood. Death was all around him, coming to claim him, too.

He jerked awake. Seconds passed before he could make sense of the stark white walls, the metal rails on the bed and the tube attached to his hand. He was in the hospital for an outpatient procedure. He wouldn't be stuck here for days on end, like last time.

Movement registered in his peripheral vision. He turned his head. A doctor was pulling his privacy curtain closed, creating a small cocoon of blue-tinted shadows. The man didn't introduce himself. Between the surgical cap and mask, only his eyes and eyebrows were visible. He gazed down at Julian with scalpel-sharp concentration.

"What's the prognosis, Doc?" Julian said, his mind fuzzy and his stomach doing somersaults. He hated being put under.

There was no response to his question.

The snap and tug of latex grated on Julian's nerves. Once the white gloves were in place, the doctor produced a syringe and needle and reached for his hand.

Something was wrong. He could feel it.

"What is that?"

Still silent, the man quickly inserted the needle into the port attached with tape to his hand. He injected the substance into the line.

"Where's my nurse?"

What was her name? He could clearly picture her youthful face, her vivid blue eyes painted with disquiet. She was familiar to him, but he couldn't pinpoint the connection.

After recapping the needle, the doctor stood and stared at him. Waiting.

Julian glanced around for a call button. There was none.

His heart began to pound. A cloud of pain spread through his chest. His lungs felt full of water. Couldn't… breathe—

"You drugged me," he sputtered, his words slurring.

A buzzing sounded in his ears. Black patches distorted his vision.

An alarm close to his bed began to go off. His blood pressure. Too high.

The man reached across and flipped a switch. Silence.

"Help—"

A gloved hand clapped over his mouth, preventing him from calling out.

He pushed at the man's arm with his uninjured hand. The surgical meds, combined with the mystery drug he'd been given, left him weak. He couldn't utilize his hand-to-hand combat skills if his body refused to cooperate.

Pray. Seek God's help.

Dizziness washed over him.

God hadn't heard him when their helo went down.

He was going to die, after all. Not a hero's death.

Murdered by a stranger. For what reason?

Sweat poured off him. He thought of his parents and three younger sisters. And his team members' loved ones, who viewed him as their last link to their fallen marines. And he thought about his nurse, whose name he couldn't remember. She had compassionate eyes. She would take a patient's death hard.

He tried again to dislodge the man's hand.

A distant shout echoed down the room. The stranger ripped through the curtain and bolted for a set of doors.

Julian clawed at the IV tube and yelled for help.

Trying to draw breath into his lungs was an impossible chore, and his heart was spasming.

He had seconds left to live.

TWO

She was going to lose him.

The heart monitor flashed a red warning. Julian was unconscious and his chest wasn't moving. No air was passing through his lips. The EKG strip showed a lethal rhythm, his heart in sustained V-tach.

Audrey called a code and dropped the bed to its lowest position. The mattress deflated to provide a hard surface. After tilting his head back, she placed her hands in the middle of his chest and began compressions.

Please, Lord Jesus, save him. If he dies, it will be my fault.

She counted in her head. Then, pinching his nose closed, she delivered rescue breaths.

Please, God...think of his family, his friends, his marines.

The code team raced in with the crash cart. She quickly told them about the intruder running free in the hospital, but there wasn't time to guess what he might've done to Julian. Dr. Menendez ran the code, evaluating the patient and clipping out orders. Another nurse unsnapped Julian's gown and positioned the pads on his chest while Audrey continued compressions. When the defibrillator level was set according to Menendez's orders, she moved aside and watched the other nurse place the paddles and shock his body.

Her gaze glued to the monitor, she willed his heart to respond.

It didn't.

She resumed CPR, putting her all into it. "Come on, Sergeant," she urged. "Fight."

"My turn," the nurse told her when Audrey would've continued.

Julian's body received another jolt of electrical current. Time seemed to stretch into eternity as Audrey waited for his rhythm to settle.

Dr. Menendez's voice cut through her preoccupation, ordering her to administer amiodarone.

She didn't immediately move. Her attention bounced between Julian's face and the monitor. *Come on. Please—*

His heart rate slowed. "Yes, that's it," Audrey murmured.

"Harris," the doctor snapped.

Audrey leaped toward the crash cart and the medications stored there. By the time the team got him stabilized and left, she was shaking. She lingered by his bedside, reassured by his restored color and the rise and fall of his chest.

Chasity walked over, her eyes troubled. Although needed in pre-op, Veronica had ordered she return until Julian left the recovery area. "He's going to be moved upstairs."

"I expected as much."

Because of his cardiac arrest, they would want to keep him under observation for a couple of days. Audrey wouldn't be able to watch over him. Maybe it was better to keep her distance, anyway. Maybe he'd be safe as long as he stayed far away from her.

She turned, and her sneaker nudged something. She crouched and, peeking beneath the bed, found a syringe. It wasn't hers. She'd discarded the one she'd used in the sharps container.

"Chasity, get Veronica."

"What's wrong?"

Pulling a single glove from the box on the counter, she used it to gingerly pick up the syringe. "Tell her we need the police." At her friend's confused look, she said, "Tell her I've found evidence the intruder left behind."

With this in their possession, they could identify the substance he'd injected into Julian and dust for fingerprints that could end this crime spree before anyone else got hurt.

Julian had had enough of hospitals. He was supposed to have gone in and gotten out in a matter of hours. Because of the incident that had nearly killed him, he'd been forced to stay longer than originally planned. Answers had proven elusive, thanks to tight-lipped administrators. He knew they were closing ranks in case he decided to pursue legal action.

At least he was home, finally, with his own bed and his own television and utter privacy.

Fitting another puzzle piece in place, he flexed the fingers of his injured hand and ground his teeth together. Two days after his procedure, the pain was dull and throbbing. Sinking against the soft leather chair, he stared at the calendar pinned to the corkboard above his desk. The serene beach photograph of Oahu's Lanikai Beach didn't distract him from the red lines slashing out every February day he'd missed work. Eight days gone. The entire month of January had been a wash.

Rolling the chair back, he stood and stalked to the apartment's compact kitchen and perused the fridge's meager contents. His appetite hadn't returned, and he wasn't interested in the assorted yogurts or chicken salad of indeterminable dates.

The doorbell chimed. Probably one of his buddies coming to cheer him up. That seemed to be the goal these days—distract Julian from the accident, remind him that he shouldn't feel guilty. His frustration building, he swung the door open and promptly forgot the words he'd been formulating.

"You." He stared at the fresh-faced brunette in his doorway. "You were at the hospital. You were my nurse."

She wiped her palms on the outside of her blue scrubs. "I'm Audrey Harris. I'm—"

"Gunny's daughter."

Julian used the door to support his weight, confusion setting in. Hers was the face dominating his memories. In fact, the expression of deep disquiet she wore now matched what he remembered of her. But was it real? Because it wasn't uncommon for him to see her around the complex. He'd been introduced to her while in a hospital bed, the *first* time he'd been admitted. His superior, Gunnery Sergeant Trent Harris, was infinitely proud of his only child. Protective, too. While Harris had been happy to introduce her to one of his marines, there was no question he expected Julian to keep his distance.

"You remember me?" Edging closer to the door frame to let a young mom with a baby on her hip pass, Audrey's big blue eyes clouded. "I didn't think you would."

He noted how expressive her eyes were, how clear and unguarded. In fact, her entire face was a billboard advertisement for her feelings. Currently, worry creased her forehead and weighted her full, pink lips into a frown.

"Did Gunny send you?"

"No. I came to your hospital room thinking you might like a break from cafeteria food." She lifted a brown paper bag. "I didn't know you'd been discharged this afternoon."

"What is that?"

"Soup. Two kinds, since I don't know your preferences."

"You brought me soup."

Why would she do that? He was technically a stranger. Unless… Was her conscience bothering her? Was she the reason he'd coded?

"Your choice of chicken noodle or vegetable beef."

He didn't feel like company, but his mom had preached the importance of good manners. Besides, he might be able to pry some answers from Audrey Harris.

"Why don't you come inside?"

As she stepped past him, her sweet scent struck him as both exotic and familiar, not quite citrusy yet not floral, either. He couldn't place it and ceased trying. The pleasure he used to find in sorting out details and mulling over conundrums eluded him now.

The nurse stopped beside his desk. She was tall and svelte. He'd seen her jogging in the park and participating in their complex's organized sports.

Her wide gaze soaked in the leather furniture, big-screen television, lava lamp and hermit crab tank. She zeroed in on the map of his home state framed above the couch.

"You're from Hawaii?"

He closed the door and stifled a sigh. He'd struggled to make small talk with friends recently, much less strangers. "Born in New York. My father's Chinese. Mom's American. We moved to Oahu when I was eight."

"Must've been wonderful to grow up in paradise."

"It has its perks." There were downsides, too, like any other place. Expensive rent. Traffic jams.

She studied the surfboard propped in the corner.

"You surf?" he asked, not really interested.

"I never learned. I preferred to play beach volleyball."

"There are plenty of people willing to teach you." At the sudden question in her eyes, he added, "For a fee. Ask the local shops."

"Maybe," she said, noncommittal.

Julian crossed to her. She had to tilt her head back to meet his gaze. Her thick waves were restrained by an elastic band. He had the inane thought that he'd never seen her hair down and wondered how long it was.

She thrust the sack at him. "I, um, hope you like at least one of them."

He accepted the offering, set it on the counter and leaned against a bar stool. *"Mahalo."*

"How's your pain level?" She gestured to the gauze encasing his arm and wrist. "Are you taking the prescribed antibiotics?"

"It's tolerable. And yes, Nurse Harris, I'm following orders. You could say I've grown accustomed to that."

"Right." Her gaze swept the length of him, taking in his marine-issued green T-shirt, black pants and socks. This wasn't a flirtatious or interested inspection. Audrey Harris was worried about him. Or worried about her job?

"You were there when I went into cardiac arrest, weren't you?"

Startled by the abrupt question, she sagged against his desk, her hip perilously close to the puzzle he'd been laboring over for weeks.

"What happened in the recovery room, Audrey?" he asked. "Why is it that, more than thirty-six hours after I was supposed to have had a routine procedure and discharge, I still don't have answers?"

"I can't say," she whispered.

He resisted the urge to use his physical stature to intimidate her. His goal wasn't to frighten her. "Did you make a mistake?" He kept his tone casual. "Did you give me the wrong medicine?"

There. A telltale flicker of guilt. "No."

Unable to contain his impatience, he straightened and took a single step toward her. "I almost died thanks to hospital error. I deserve to know the truth."

"It wasn't hospital error," she blurted, popping up from the desk.

"Oh?"

"Someone masquerading as hospital staff entered recovery and administered a lethal dose of epinephrine."

"What?"

"We don't know his identity. The police weren't able to get fingerprints off the syringe. They're combing through security footage, but there are many areas of the building that aren't covered." Her dark brows snapped together. "I'm sorry, Julian."

Vague memories of a man wearing a surgical mask emerged. He hadn't spoken, but the intent in his eyes had unsettled Julian. He'd worn latex gloves and had a short ponytail.

"I saw him."

"You did? What does he look like? If you can give a description—"

"His face was obscured. The curtain was drawn and the light behind my bed turned off."

"I turned it off so you could rest," she admitted, biting her lip.

He paced to the window. There wasn't much activity in the parking lot below or the public park bordering their Jacksonville complex. This was the dinner hour, when people would be sharing meals with their families. He ignored the pang of loneliness. What right did he have to feel lonely? His team members, his brothers—Paulson, Akins, Rossello and Cook—didn't have the luxury.

"I don't have enemies." His adversaries inhabited foreign soil. They didn't know him by name. They only knew his organization—United States Marine Corps Force Reconnaissance. "This can't be connected to me."

"I should go. I've already said too much."

Her shoulders were hunched and her mouth pinched. She was hiding something. Blocking her exit, he said, "Where were you when the intruder got to me?"

The color drained from her face. "I had another patient. She was ill. I stepped out to get her a cup of ice." Her lashes swept down. "When I returned, I saw the curtain drawn. I saw his outline. I tried to stop him and would've gone after him, but you'd gone into V-tach. I had to begin CPR at once—"

"You saved my life?" Julian attempted to picture her springing into heroine mode. She hadn't caused his brush with death. She'd kept him from succumbing to it.

"I did what I was trained to do."

He recognized the refusal to take credit. Audrey Harris, RN, didn't view her job as extraordinary. Sometimes force-recon marines got their names in the paper or received medals from government officials. Like Audrey, Julian had been trained for specific tasks and taught to react to emergencies. He didn't think of himself as special because of it.

Her phone beeped. She took it from her pocket and, reading the screen, frowned. "I have to go."

"I have more questions."

"I'm in apartment 478, on the other side of the elevators and vending machines. If you have any questions regarding your recovery, come by anytime."

The emergence of stubborn resolve surprised him. He

hadn't seen past the very real apprehension cloaking her. But she was the daughter of a career marine. What had he expected? A wilting flower?

Deliberately stepping around him, she reached for the doorknob.

"You should know I don't give up easily," he said.

Audrey paused. "Get some rest, Sergeant Tan."

In other words, focus on complete healing instead of pursuing this mystery.

When she'd left, he returned to his puzzle but had trouble concentrating. Audrey knew more than she was willing to share. Was she worried about compromising her position at the hospital? Or was it something far more serious?

Either way, he was determined to discover the truth.

THREE

Audrey tugged at the wet material clinging to her skin and grimaced. Her foot had gotten caught on the hospital bed wheel, and she'd stumbled, spilling apple juice down her front. If it had been water, she would've let it air-dry. But the juice would start to smell foul. And it was sticky.

She headed for the door. "I'm going to get a new set of scrubs from supply."

Veronica, who'd hovered like a thundercloud since the incident, looked up from her handheld device. Her garish red lips formed a disgruntled slash. "Hurry up." She tilted her head at the unoccupied beds. "Our ten o'clock knee replacement is almost done."

In the hallway, she removed her cap and tucked it in her pocket. She readjusted the band holding her hair in place as she navigated the brightly lit hall. A security guard passed and nodded in greeting. There hadn't been any more problems with her patients, for which she was grateful. Almost losing Julian had rattled her. He didn't play a role in her life, but there was something about the stoic marine that touched a chord inside. Maybe it was the fact he'd ignored his own safety to pull the others out of that wrecked helicopter.

His striking looks had nothing to do with it, she reassured herself. Neither did his brooding demeanor or the loneliness and grief he tried to hide from the world.

Pushing thoughts of the sergeant from her mind, she left the surgical unit, passed through the central lobby area and entered a stairwell that would take her down to the basement level. Their unit's supply room had run out of space months ago. Until they could rearrange stock or create more storage, overflow was located in a secondary area that didn't see much traffic.

Muted orange-yellow light spilled down the concrete stairs, drawing attention to gouges in the cement walls and the stair rail's peeling paint. At the bottom, she shouldered open the heavy door. A vinegary odor emanating from the basement labs greeted her in the narrow hallway. She didn't pass a single person as she followed the worn, cracked tiles to the room at the end. Inside, she flipped the switch. Only about half of the overhead lights flickered on, leaving much of the high shelving systems in shadow.

"Great," she muttered. With no windows to admit natural light, it was going to take time to dig through the scrubs to find her size.

She wove through the network of short aisles to reach the rear wall. Rounding the last section, Audrey nearly jumped out of her skin when a loud crash clattered right behind her. Her hand pressed to her thrumming heart, she pivoted and saw that her foot had dislodged a mop propped against the wall. Crouching down, she grabbed the wooden handle off the hard tiles and set it right again.

Another sound reached her, then…the grinding of sand beneath a rubber shoe sole.

The hair on her arms stood at attention. Audrey did a complete turn in the tight passage, between wooden shelves and a painted block wall.

"Hello?"

The thought of the person who'd invaded the recovery room flashed in her mind. Had the thief decided his current methods weren't working? After all, she hadn't quit. Hadn't been fired. Hadn't remained silent.

Had he switched targets?

Audrey remained frozen for long minutes, her ears straining for out-of-place clues that she wasn't alone. There was nothing. Hurrying to the stacks, she sorted through shirts and pants for her size, too distracted to worry about tidying up after herself.

"There. Done."

A presence registered behind her before she could turn around to leave. Measured breathing. The rustle of clothing.

Adrenaline charged through her system too late. Something hard and unyielding came up and over her head and pressed against her throat, cutting off her air supply. Silencing her.

The scrubs slipped from her fingers. Reaching up, she gripped the stick. *Can't breathe.*

She couldn't dislodge it. He was immovable, her captor, his arms and chest forming a vise around her.

Dots danced in her vision. She struggled. Writhed. Kicked. Her lungs stretched to the bursting point.

Audrey reached up to claw at his face. If she could gouge his eyes—

He increased the pressure. Pain was a scream lodged in her throat.

As consciousness ebbed, thoughts of her dad filled her with sadness. The loss of Audrey's mother had almost destroyed him. What would burying his only child do?

Her body was growing limp. She was out of time.

A tear dripped down her cheek.

Shouts pierced the black cloud. Suddenly, the arms around her went slack. He let the mop fall and spun away from her.

Audrey swayed and fell to her knees. A scuffle ensued between her attacker and would-be rescuer. In the murky light, she recognized the stark white dressing on the second man's arm.

"Julian," she gasped.

He shouldn't be here. Shouldn't be confronting an attacker in his condition, most likely the same man who tried to kill him mere days ago.

Julian blocked the other man's fist with his good arm, and then used his leg to land a forceful kick to his opponent's gut. When the man's body glanced off the shelf, Julian tackled him. The pair hit the floor in a blur of blows and deflections, their grunts loud in her ears.

Her attacker was clad in black. A ski mask obscured his face. His greater bulk made him a fearsome foe. However, he was less agile than the marine. Julian quickly gained control of the situation. He pinned the man on his stomach and wedged his knee against his spine.

After removing a pistol tucked beneath the man's suitcoat, he cast a searching glance in her direction. "You okay?"

Audrey belatedly realized she was still on the floor. She pushed to her feet and prayed her legs would hold her.

"I'm good." Her throat ached, and her head throbbed with the stirrings of a headache, but she was alive. Thanks to him.

Her relief was short-lived. In a burst of energy, her attacker leveraged himself up, slamming his head into Julian's. His beefy arm swung wildly and connected with Julian's cheek. The double blows dazed him long enough for the masked man to get up and flee.

Julian's gaze kept returning to the angry welts that marred Audrey's delicate skin. He didn't want to contemplate the possible outcome of this morning's attack if he hadn't come for a post-op checkup and spotted her passing the gift shop. He hadn't planned to pester her with his questions, since she was on duty. But then he'd seen the goon in a dress suit enter the stairwell, and he'd decided to follow his instincts. The goon hadn't been wearing the ski mask in the general area of the hospital, but Julian hadn't gotten a clear view of his face.

He eased the tissue from his cheek and tossed it in the bin. The cut wasn't deep. Still, it irked him. Weeks of desk duty had made him soft. If this had happened before January, he'd have subdued that guy and not suffered a single bruise. He wouldn't have let himself be distracted by a pretty woman, either.

Julian inwardly cringed at his stupidity. The guys would have a hearty laugh over this one—

No, they wouldn't. Because they were dead. Paulson, Akins, Rossello, Cook. Upstanding, honorable men. The best of the best.

Suppressing a tide of grief, he refocused on Audrey. Instantly, he knew she needed a break from the repetitive—and at this stage, pointless—questions.

Pushing off the wall, he stalked to where she perched on the edge of a hard, plastic seat. Her head was bowed.

"We're done here," Julian stated.

Both Audrey and the security member gaped at him.

"We need more information—"

"No, you don't. There's nothing more to tell." Worried about her enlarged pupils and ashen complexion, he held out his hand. "Come with me, Audrey."

Placing her trembling hand in his, she allowed him to lead her out of the office. He ushered her to the nearest exit, which emptied into a courtyard with massive plant pots and a koi pond in one corner. The early morning air had a crisp bite to it. Good, because she needed to cool off physically and emotionally.

She sat on the bench he indicated and stared at nothing. Julian crouched in front of her.

He touched her knee. "Can I get you a soda? Coffee?"

Clasping her hands tightly in lap, she shook her head. The elastic band holding her hair was about to slip free.

"You, um—" He leaned forward and gingerly removed the blue band, registering the sensation of her silky hair against his skin. Her alluring, summery scent washed over him. Again, he had a strong recollection of something tied to his childhood. "Here you go."

She closed her hand over the band. Her shiny tresses spilled past her shoulders, tumbling waves of rich sable.

"What about a cherry slushy?" he said. "The cafeteria might have one."

Her lips parted. "How do you know about that?"

"Don't freak out. I've shared a few elevator rides with you. More often than not, you have a slushy from the gas station, and cherry has a distinctive color."

When she continued to stare at him with that arrested expression, he moved to sit beside her. "Look, I'm trained to notice details. In some instances, it can lead to capturing a terrorist or preventing an attack. In others, it means I know what my neighbors like to drink after a long shift. That's not a habit I can turn off when I'm out of uniform."

Sighing, she swept her hair behind her shoulder. "I have a weakness for cherry-flavored Jolly Ranchers, too."

He felt a smile forming. "Good to know."

She studied his cheek before cutting a glance at his arm. "Please tell me you didn't reinjure your arm."

"I didn't reinjure my arm."

Her eyes darkened. "You saved me."

"I was in the right place at the right time."

"I thank God for it."

"What's going on, Audrey?"

She bit her lip and shrugged. He was tempted to walk away. He'd suffered no lasting effects from his ordeal, and Audrey Harris was none of his concern. The one thing stopping him from escorting her back to security was the thought of his younger sisters. If any one of them was facing a threat and he wasn't around to help, he'd want someone to step up to the plate.

Plus, she'd saved his life. So what if he'd done the same for her? He didn't believe in calling things even. He owed her a debt of gratitude that couldn't be repaid.

He tried again. "You can't tell me these attacks aren't connected."

Indecision played out across her face. Her knuckles went white.

"I couldn't help my team," he said quietly. "But maybe I can help you."

Her surprise mirrored his own. Why had he said that? He didn't like thinking about what had happened, much less put it into words.

"There's a thief in the hospital," she said in a rush. "Someone's been taking partially used ampules of narcotics to feed their addiction. They might also be watering down patient doses and taking the rest for themselves. I'm not sure."

Actions with serious, perhaps even fatal, consequences. "You told your supervisor?"

"And some of my coworkers. Soon after, there were issues with my patients. Nothing life-threatening until you." Her expression turned bleak. "This person must have a terrible addiction to feed."

Julian sagged against the bench. The average drug user wouldn't go to such extreme lengths to quell an investigation. It seemed to him that Audrey had gotten herself into something far more sinister. But what?

"Does your father know?"

She bolted to her feet and stared down at him. "He knows nothing, and that's the way it stays."

"I've served under him for more than a year. Gunny is a private man, but I have learned several things. Laziness and carelessness are his top pet peeves. He hates surprises. Can't function on less than four cups of coffee a day, and he believes his only daughter hung the moon."

"If my dad found out, he'd try to force me to quit. He still sees me as a helpless little girl." Worry pinched her mouth. "Please don't tell him."

"You're putting me in an untenable position. You know that, right?"

"I can handle this on my own."

"Really?" He stood up. This close, he could see the contrast between her irises' navy outer ring and the azure blue interior. Like the varying shades of the Pacific surrounding his island home. "What's your plan?"

She licked her lips. "First off, I won't be going into the supply room alone." When he didn't comment, she continued. "I'll be extra vigilant, both here and outside the hospital."

"You think this will go away on its own."

"That's what I'm praying will happen."

Prayer hadn't made a single difference when that helo went down. He'd begged God to let his team live. His pleas had been in vain.

She spoke again, temporarily halting his descent into bitterness. "You're a good listener, Sergeant Tan. I thank you for that. Now I'm asking you to respect my decision not to involve my dad."

"I won't volunteer the information."

At his unspoken warning, she frowned. "And you won't give him any reason to ask questions, I hope."

Through the floor-to-ceiling windows behind her, Julian spotted a male nurse headed for the courtyard. He burst outside in a cloud of anger. "Veronica said to go home, Audrey."

"Home? I don't finish until seven."

The veins bulged at his temple. Older than Audrey by about a decade, the man looked like he led a rough life. Bloodshot eyes, reddened nose, sallow complexion. His head was shaved to call less attention to his bald spot. He was thin to the point of gauntness.

"I'll have to work alone this shift," he spat, dismissing Julian with a sneer. "You need to get your act together. If you don't, I'm going to Mr. Harper."

The door slammed behind him. Audrey had grown pale again.

"One of your coworkers?"

"Frank Russo."

"And Mr. Harper? Who's he?"

"Hospital president."

He didn't know her well enough to assume that she was innocent, but he'd developed keen instincts when it came to a person's character. His gut said she was the sort of girl who put a high priority on others' comfort. Otherwise, why choose a career that held zero glamour and demanded she give her all to the well-being of strangers?

"You've done nothing wrong, Audrey."

Her mouth twisted. "Problem is, I can't prove it."

Not convinced leaving her alone was a good idea, Julian accompanied her to the cafeteria. As they didn't have a slushy machine, she settled for coffee. He watched as she doctored it.

"I'll follow you home when you're ready," he said.

"I'm going upstairs to speak with Veronica." She took

a small sip to taste and added another packet of sugar. "There's no reason why I shouldn't work today."

While her color had returned to normal and the welt across her throat looked less angry, she was jumpy, as her gaze performed frequent sweeps of the room.

"Give me your phone."

"Why?"

"I want you to have my number, just in case."

"That's not necessary." At the register, she swiped her employee ID and thanked the cashier.

"I insist."

She reluctantly did as he asked. When he'd finished inputting the information, she tucked it back into her pocket. "I don't plan on calling you."

"I hope you don't have to."

"I know why you're doing this."

"Oh, yeah?"

"Because of my dad. And because you have a warrior mind-set. You see a problem, you fix it. You see someone in trouble, you make it your business to help. Like you said before, you don't know how to turn off the marine and be a regular guy."

All those things may be true, but he suspected there was more to his drive to help her. There was something different about her, an elusive quality that intrigued him. He didn't want to be intrigued. Didn't want to notice her compassionate eyes, her cute nose or kind mouth. He certainly didn't want to catch her looking at him like he was that word the newspapers had thrown around. He wasn't a hero.

"Speaking of problems, we're about to have one."

She glanced over her shoulder to the main set of double doors and gasped. "What is he doing here?"

Trent Harris strode into the dining area alongside a male friend. They were deep in conversation and hadn't spotted them yet. Although out of uniform, Trent had the military look, his silver hair buzzed short and his physique honed from years of service. He exuded an undeniable air of authority.

"I forgot Dad meets with some of the board of directors this time of year to plan the annual charity golf tournament. I can't let him see me like this," she said, gesturing to her neck. "I'll slip out the side exit."

"Audrey—"

"Please, he has enough to worry about with work. All those men lost…he's taking it hard. Maybe not as hard as you are—" She broke off, her eyes pleading with him. "I can't burden him with this. Not now."

Julian didn't agree, but what say did he have in her choices? "Fine. Go."

"Thank you." She dodged tables and garbage receptacles and rushed out the door. He was watching her retreating form through the large windows separating the cafeteria and hallway when his superior approached.

"Sergeant Tan." His eyes—the same bold hue as his daughter's—gleamed with speculation. "What are you doing here?"

Harris's friend continued into the food service area. "I had a post-op checkup."

One broad eyebrow arched in silent question.

"It's healing on schedule. I'll report for work Monday." Not for his usual duties, he thought bitterly. They'd planted him at an admin desk until the unit doctor decided to return him to full duty or trot him before a medical board for retirement consideration. Before the accident, he would've prayed for God to restore the career he loved. He didn't bother now.

"If you need more sick time, call Staff Sergeant Webb."

His lips pressed into a thin line. "Now, why don't you explain to me what you were doing with my daughter?"

Julian controlled his reaction. He'd begun to think Harris hadn't seen her. "Audrey was getting coffee, sir. We talked."

"About?"

None of your business, he wanted to say. But he respected the man. Julian would go so far as to say he admired him. "My recovery. Your daughter is very conscientious."

"Hmm."

He stifled the urge to squirm beneath the stare that would have lesser men spilling all their secrets. "Looks like your friend has his food. I'll see you in the office."

"Tan."

The single word had the effect of a snapped whip. Julian stopped short.

"I like you, but I'm envisioning a quiet, stable life for my daughter. I'm hoping I'll get a doctor or lawyer for a son-in-law."

"I understand, sir." Marines need not apply, especially force-recon marines. They had a reputation for being rougher and wilder than the rest. Not that Julian had done anything to earn such a reputation. "I have no intention of dating Audrey."

He nodded, seemingly appeased. "I'm glad we're on the same page."

Julian left the hospital feeling dissatisfied. Thoughts of Audrey trailed him the rest of the day. He had a feeling this wasn't over. But Harris had warned him off, and the woman herself didn't want his help or protection.

He didn't need the distraction, anyway. Getting his old life back had to be his main focus.

FOUR

Her apartment door was ajar.

The mental and physical exhaustion that had rendered her almost dizzy during the drive home was instantly forgotten as she touched her fingertips to the black painted wood. She'd locked it this morning. She always locked it. Thanks to her dad's infamous lectures, "safety" could be her middle name.

Audrey bent to examine the knob and doorjamb and didn't see any obvious damage. But then, anyone wanting to get in without alerting the neighbors could've used something as simple as a credit card. Her throat ached as memories of the storage-room attack pressed in. Had it only been a matter of hours since a stranger had attempted to murder her? She stared at the door, a tsunami of uncertainty building inside. Had he discovered her home address and decided to try again when she was alone and there was less chance of interference?

The urge to run to Julian's apartment was strong. She'd insisted she wouldn't call him. She hadn't said anything about not pounding on his door.

The slim chance that a maintenance man had made an unscheduled visit kept her in place.

Taking a steadying breath, she pushed the door inward and was granted an unobstructed view of the entryway and short hallway that emptied into the dining nook. Her knees threatened to buckle. Late evening sun slanted through the patio doors, glinting on bits of glass and broken picture frames. Shoes formed haphazard piles on the linoleum—they'd been yanked out of the storage cubicle tucked against the wall.

Audrey didn't pause to consider her options. Spinning on her heel, she jogged down the hall, half-expecting to be ambushed from behind.

She pounded on Julian's door. From this distance, she couldn't see her apartment. Her assailant could use the opportunity to slip out undetected. Or he could still be hiding in her closet, behind her shower curtain or beneath her bed...

The door swung open, revealing a sleep-tousled marine. At the sight of her, he snapped to attention. "Audrey."

"I woke you, didn't I? I promised not to bother you with my problems, but my door was open and my stuff is everywhere—"

She broke off when he left her in the doorway and disappeared into what she assumed was his bedroom. When he returned, he had a sleek black gun in his grip and there was no trace of fatigue in his hardened face. He didn't spare her a glance as he strode past her into the hall. This, she realized, was a force-recon marine in action, focus narrowed on the potential threat.

Audrey followed, her gaze glued to the surf-shop insignia stretched across his broad, muscular back. Reservations kicked in. What was she thinking? Mere days ago he'd hovered near death. She'd fought to keep him alive, and now she was sending him straight into danger.

He was about to cross the threshold when she spoke. "Maybe this isn't a good idea. I should contact the police."

Julian held a finger to his lips and continued into her apartment, sweeping the rooms one by one. The sight of her home in chaos, and the knowledge that a stranger had invaded her space and touched her things, made her feel sick and violated. It didn't help that Julian was seeing her life laid bare.

Returning to the living room, he tucked the gun into his waistband. "He's gone."

Audrey bent to retrieve a crumpled photograph of herself and Seth off the floor. The image was one of her favorites, taken at a local shrimp festival, where they'd eaten their weight in fried shrimp and hush puppies and lounged on the riverbank listening to live bands. A month later, a cancer diagnosis had upended their innocent world.

Julian's fingertips grazed her arm. "You shouldn't touch anything. Not until the police have dusted for prints."

There were questions in his eyes that she was thankful he didn't put a voice to. The lump in her throat grew, and she nodded mutely. While he called the police and gave a brief report, she wandered through the rooms again, impatient to restore order and erase the evidence of the intrusion.

He rejoined her in the kitchen, frowning at the swirl of ground spices on the countertops and pots and pans on the tiles. "A unit is en route. They'll want to know if anything's missing."

A gasp ripped from her lips. How could she have forgotten?

Brushing past him, she hurried to her bedroom and, dropping to her knees in the closet, reached for the decorative boxes shoved in the corner. They weren't in a neat stack anymore.

Her heart sank. He'd found her hiding place.

"Audrey?"

"My journal." She frantically rifled through the contents discarded on the thick carpet. "It's not here. He took it."

Moving closer to crouch beside her, he rested his hand

on her shoulder. The connection grounded her. Kept her from flying apart. "What's in the journal?"

She ended her futile search and twisted to meet his gaze.

"Evidence."

Julian stood between the entertainment center and couch, out of the way but within reach should Audrey need him. He watched her speak with the Jacksonville police officers—one young male and a thirtyish female—while the crime-scene guys dusted for prints. She'd had a nightmare of a day, yet she exuded admirable composure. Still in her scrubs, her glossy hair in an intricate braid, she stood with her sneakers far apart and her arms folded over her chest. Her tone was even, her words succinct. Only her eyes bore witness of her distress.

For a second there on the closet floor, he'd nearly given in to the need to fold her in his arms and comfort her. He'd stifled it. Audrey hadn't reached out to him for emotional support. He wasn't sure he could manage to shoulder anyone else's hurt. It was taking all his energy to contain his own.

The male officer looked up from his handheld device. "This journal of yours? What information does it contain?"

"Dates. Patient names." She tugged on her hospital ID. "I detailed each and every instance of missing supplies and narcotics, as well as the wrongly administered medications and patient reactions."

"Did you keep a second copy on your laptop or flash drive?"

She glanced at her ruined laptop, smashed on the floor. Her rose-tinted mouth dipped into a grimace. "I didn't think to. I should have. I didn't imagine it would progress to this…"

The officers exchanged a significant glance. The journal was likely already destroyed, and without an electronic copy, her claims couldn't be substantiated.

"We're going to speak to the residents on this floor. Someone might've seen something suspicious or heard unusual noises. We'll also go over the building's security-camera footage."

They left soon after, along with the crime-scene officers, and promised to reach out if they discovered anything useful.

He joined her in the entryway. "I'd like to help clean up. I can work in the kitchen and bathrooms." The least personal spaces, which he expected she'd prefer.

"I've taken up enough of your time." Avoiding his gaze, she started pairing shoes and sliding them into the cubicle slots.

"My calendar's swiped clean these days." His choice. "You'll be saving me from bingeing on home-decorating shows."

Lifting her head, she stared at him.

"Trust me," he said, "I know all I need to know about accent walls and upcycling."

Her lips lifted in a semblance of a smile. "You sure about that? There's usually a new style concept waiting to be sprung on the masses."

He picked up a delicate high-heeled sandal and handed it to her. "I'm sure."

After he helped her finish the shoes, they worked in separate areas. As he organized her kitchen cabinets, his thoughts drifted to that photo. Who was the young man who'd had his arm slung proudly around Audrey's shoulders? Where was he now?

It's none of your business, Tan.

He had no personal interest in Gunny's daughter. He had no interest in romance, period. On occasion, he'd ask out a girl for a casual day of surfing or sailing, but he made it clear up front that he wasn't looking for commitment. He'd already disappointed his father with his decision to forego college and enlist in the US Marine Corps. Trying and failing at the sacred institution of marriage would further damage Chin Tan's opinion of his only son. Military marriages faced myriad challenges. When clandestine, dangerous missions were the norm, a husband and wife had to have a steel-tight bond to weather daily life.

Shaking his head at the direction of his thoughts, he refocused on the task at hand and moved to the guest bathroom. After more than an hour of cleaning, Audrey's apartment held no signs of the break-in. A different layout than his, the space was feminine and breezy without being cluttered. Her sense of humor showed in her choice of wall art, which mostly consisted of whimsical animal paintings in vibrant colors. Unlike him, she'd taken the time to hang curtains and assemble pillows and rugs. He liked her style.

His stomach rumbled, and she heard it.

"I haven't had a chance to shop for groceries, or I'd offer to cook supper." Pulling off her ID, she dropped it into a ceramic fish-shaped dish. "How about I order takeout? Do you like Italian food? There's a new place down the street."

He was tempted. If they shared a meal, he'd have the chance to ask questions, to glean insight into her personality. That was the reason he had to say no. While her outward beauty attracted him, her innate kindness and sweetness of spirit appealed to his soul. Dangerous territory. Didn't take long in his line of work to become hard and cynical. Digging in to God's Word with a trusted group of military men had prevented him from becoming completely callous. He'd had trouble praying since the accident, however, and he certainly hadn't opened his Bible.

"*Mahalo* for the offer, but I'll pass."

Was it his imagination, or did her shoulders slump a little?

"Maybe another time," she said, her gaze direct and her voice even.

"You should stay with a friend tonight."

"Then I'd have to explain why I need a place to crash, and I don't want to drag anyone else into my mess." Sinking onto the curved sofa arm, Audrey smoothed a wisp of dark hair off her forehead. It was a weary gesture that again evoked the urge to soothe and comfort. He strangled it. "He already got what he wanted. Without those notes, I have nothing to stand on."

Julian took a few steps closer. "Your father—"

"Stop." Her spine stiffened. "We aren't going there."

With effort, he held back his arguments. This was her life, her choices. "I wish you'd reconsider, but in the meantime, I'm here if you need me. Call. Text. Knock. I'll help in any way I can."

"Thank you, Julian." With a sigh, she stood and led the way to her door, effectively escorting him out.

As he walked back to his apartment, he was surprised by how much he regretted not agreeing to eat with her. Had to be because he was worried this guy wouldn't be satisfied with burying evidence and wouldn't rest until he'd buried Audrey, too.

FIVE

Audrey wasn't answering her phone. Julian knocked on her door again, willing her to open it. He'd spent the night tossing and turning, entertaining various scenarios that made it impossible to sleep. She shouldn't be alone. Alone, she was at the mercy of a would-be killer. He never should've agreed to keep this from her father. Gunny Harris lived for two things—his only child and the Corps, in that order. The emotional wounds would be beyond repair if anything happened to her. Harris would be a broken man, and Julian would be to blame.

He took the elevator to the ground level and entered the parking lot, tension tightening his shoulders at the sight of her older model Jetta. Cheering and whistles reached him from the activity fields between the apartment building and gym. A volleyball game was in progress. He wove through the vehicles to reach the spectators—out to enjoy the unseasonably warm weather—and spotted her at the net. The vise in his chest loosened.

She was fine.

She didn't need him.

He started to turn away, to return to his apartment and another dull morning, which would stretch into a duller afternoon, when she leaped into the air and spiked the ball. He was accustomed to seeing her in hospital scrubs. Today she sported a white T-shirt, red shorts and red, black and white sneakers. Slightly taller than average, with a lean torso and long, tanned legs, Audrey was a neat package of athleticism and grace.

Julian drifted closer to watch the game. By the time it

was over, he was certain she'd played on a college-level team. He would've put the question to her if he hadn't been waylaid by a buddy from church who wasn't shy in asking when Julian planned to return.

When he looked around again, most of the players and spectators had dispersed. Audrey must've returned to her place. Ignoring the odd sense of disappointment, he walked past the line of cars closest to the field. The one in the last slot caught his attention.

It was a sleek Mercedes with blacked-out windows. Because of its price tag, the vehicle alone was cause for a second look. The owner aroused more than mere curiosity. Steroid-sized muscles strained his designer suit. His face was mostly hidden by sunglasses and a bushy mustache. Because of his career, Julian had interacted with enough dirtbags to recognize the type. What was he doing at their complex? Running down some idiot who'd borrowed money from the wrong people? Checking up on a low-level drug pusher?

Their complex wouldn't be considered ultraluxurious, but neither was it low-end. The monthly fee was affordable for single professionals and young married couples, and out of reach for the type of resident who'd dally in petty crime.

Unless...

Foreboding niggled at the base of his skull. What if the man was here for an altogether different reason? One involving a hospital cover-up?

Audrey carried the sack of volleyballs to the storage closet, her mind on a certain spectator who had shaken her concentration. She hadn't been surprised to see Julian on the edge of the crowd, despite the fact he hadn't shown interest in group activities before. Honor spilled through his veins, and duty was etched in his DNA. He'd assumed the role of protector because she was his superior's daughter. She was an obligation, plain and simple. She'd been reminded of that truth last night, when he'd quickly shut down her offer. Sharing a meal would've meant they were more than passing acquaintances brought together by outrageous circumstances. Sharing a meal would've meant he was interested in getting to know her better. He wasn't.

She embraced the disappointment, the sting of rejection. It was a timely reminder—her heart wasn't ready for a relationship. Not even casual friendship, which she'd seen other women do but hadn't ever experienced herself. She and Seth had been full-on serious from the start. The sad part? Audrey was fairly certain Julian would make a wonderful friend.

She moved past mirrored walls and stacks of barbells. The quiet unnerved her. The exercise gym was unusually empty, no doubt on account of the unusually warm weather.

Skirting the large, complex pulley-and-weight station, she entered the rear hallway, then set down the sack and unlocked the double closet doors with the key she'd gotten from the main office. A creaking sound echoed through the gym. Breath hitching, she whirled around and nearly stumbled over the balls. The lights were off, and shadows lurked on either end of the hall.

"Hello?"

The men's bathroom was to her left, the women's on her right. Maybe they were occupied.

Wishing she didn't have a reason to be paranoid, Audrey entered the walk-in closet and emptied the balls into a metal container. Then she hung the sack on a wall hook. Impatient to be outside and around other people, she closed the doors with more force than necessary. She tried to jam the key into the knob and accidentally dropped it. When she bent to retrieve it, she heard heavy breathing behind her.

Panicked, she shot upward and spun around in time to see a giant man in a suit swinging a barbell at her head. She tried to dodge it. The blow landed on her upper arm, knocking her sideways. Pain radiated through her.

Pushing off the doorjamb, she sprinted past him. He put out a foot. She went sprawling face-first onto the thin carpet. Rolling beneath a weight bench, she screamed when the barbell slammed into the cushioned seat, the force sending vibrations through the metal legs. Terror exploded inside. This man was going to crush her skull with that thing.

Audrey flipped to her stomach and crawled from beneath the bench. Leaping to her feet, she raced for the nearest exit, only to skid to a stop. A second man—younger and slighter but no less a threat—blocked her escape. There was no going around him.

She was trapped.

A scream ripped through the narrow room, and it wasn't hers.

Time seemed to screech to a halt. At the far end, another volleyball player stood frozen in her tracks. The goon with the twenty-five-pound weight glued to his fist snarled at his partner. "You were supposed to lock this place down."

"Must've missed one," the other retorted.

Weight Guy charged toward her.

"Laney, run!" Audrey shouted.

When the petite redhead didn't react, Audrey raced after her attacker, vaulted onto the guy's back and latched onto his thick neck.

Laney's eyes bugged.

"Go, go!"

At last, she bolted. Her retreating footsteps were like nails in a coffin. Audrey was now alone with two attackers. Not ordinary men. Muscle-bound henchmen with eyes dead to human compassion. Coldhearted killers.

Trying to cut off his air supply was impossible. The room spun as he turned a circle and slammed her into the weight station. Sharp metal jarred her shoulder blades and spine and dug into her flesh. Her head snapped back.

He shifted, and she slid to her knees. Spots danced in her vision. Her stomach lurched.

In an instant, the second man was there. "Go get the other one. Conner's still at the car. He can help you. I'll deal with the nurse."

She heard a clink above her. A long, rubber-encased handle clattered to the floor nearby. Before she could summon the energy to flee, a beefy hand closed over her neck and hauled her to her feet.

Audrey gagged and clawed at his grip. His pale eyes drilled into hers. Ruthless. Merciless.

"You've caused my boss enough trouble," he growled. "No more."

Before she could guess what he was about, he'd pushed her beneath the high lat muscle pull-down and looped twin cables around her neck. He reached behind her, and she heard the slide of the metal clip in the thin, black weights attached to the pull-down bar. The wire went taut, pinching her skin, forcing her onto her tiptoes.

"Four hundred pounds should do it."

Her mind went blank. As soon as he let go of her, the cables stretched, the weights slapped into place and lifted her several inches off the floor.

She dangled in midair, unable to breathe. She kicked and squirmed.

Pain ripped through her. Her neck felt like it was about to separate from her body.

Please, God. Help. I'm not ready—

The bald, gold-jewelry-draped goon smirked. "No use fighting it, babe."

He crossed his arms and watched her struggle with frightening impassivity. His was the last face she'd ever see. A cruel, evil being taking delight in her fight to cling to life.

Her lungs strained for oxygen. A familiar sensation.

Was he the same one who'd attempted to strangle her at the hospital?

Audrey grew light-headed. Her thoughts became disjointed.

She ceased moving. The agony was too great.

She closed her eyes and concentrated on her dad's face. He'd loved her well. She would die thinking about him, not the end of unfulfilled dreams.

Julian left the flashy car and mystery man behind and was retracing his steps when a redhead burst through the gym's side door, her face a white mask of disbelief. Her frantic gaze locked onto him.

"Audrey," she gasped, chest heaving. "Two men... I—I—"

He gripped her shoulders. "Go to the office and call the police."

"Police." Her throat convulsed. "Right."

"Walk, don't run. Act casual." He jerked his head toward the Mercedes tucked close to the apartment-building entrance. "Avoid that area. Take the long way around the outdoor pool."

"Okay."

Julian couldn't delay. He'd have to trust she would follow his instructions and avoid the man who might very well be the getaway driver. Unsheathing his weapon from the ankle holster beneath his pants, he entered the gym and searched the space behind the check-in counter. The tiny office was closed on the weekends, and the locked door suggested no one was inside.

His ears strained for sounds of struggle. The silence weighed on him. Blanking his mind to possible implications, he left the counter area and passed the water fountains and childcare room. Up ahead, treadmills and elliptical machines were parked in front of mounted televisions. There were no mirrors in that section that could give him a glimpse of Audrey's situation.

The adrenaline priming his body for confrontation left no room for fear. His training ruled his actions and decisions. So when a suited man turned the corner and headed straight for him, Julian fired two shots without blinking, one for each kneecap.

Curses blistered the air as the man went down. Quickly divesting the man of his single weapon, Julian flattened against the wall and peered around the corner. Kneecap Guy's cohort was on his way to investigate. That didn't faze him.

What caused ice-cold dread to spread through him was the sight of Audrey's limp form dangling from the weight station. He couldn't be too late. Not again.

Stepping fully into the exercise area, he trained his weapon and shot the man's gun hand. Hissing in agony, he dropped his weapon and, after a second's indecision, escaped through the side door.

Julian kicked the gun under a stack of barbells for the authorities to retrieve later. He reached Audrey and immediately took her weight, positioning her against his shoulder to lessen the tension on her neck. "Audrey, can you hear me?"

He glanced up into her motionless face. Her cheeks and lips still held the blush of color. A good sign. Images of the burning wreckage and the faces of his unresponsive team members poked at his composure. He had asked

them the same question. Over and over until his voice
had gone hoarse.

*Can you hear me? Wake up. Hold on. The ambulance
is coming.*

He shook his head to dislodge the memories. *Focus,
Tan. Audrey's life depends upon your actions.*

Dragging a weight bench over with his foot, he positioned her shoes on the soft pad and, not letting go, climbed
onto it and unwound the cables with one hand. The flut-
ter of her heartbeat and small, panting breaths filled him
with relief. He kept his ears open for foreign sounds. If
the guy at the Mercedes was indeed part of the operation,
he'd come to see what was taking his buddies so long.

Finally, when he had her free, he climbed down, hoisted
her into his arms and dashed for the women's bathroom.
The locker rooms with toilet stalls were in the adjoining
indoor-pool section. These consisted of one-room units
with locks on the doors.

He yanked open the door, ignoring the responding ache
in his injured wrist, and gently laid her on the tiles against
the wall opposite the sink. After sliding the bolt into place,
he returned to her side and did a quick scan for obvious
injuries. He would've liked to hold her, to cushion her
head in his lap, but he didn't want to exacerbate any hidden injuries. Instead, he smoothed his fingers over her
forehead and down her cheek.

His pulse raced when she arced toward the caress.

"Audrey, you're safe now."

A groan escaped her parted lips. She reached up and
would've touched her throat, but he clasped her hand to
prevent germs from entering the open scratches. There
weren't many. Mostly the welts were puffy and red. Her
eyes flew open.

"Julian." Her brow knitted. "How did we get in here?"

He explained about the thug outside with his flashy ride, as well as her volleyball teammate.

Terror filled her eyes. "Is Laney safe?"

"I sent her on a roundabout course to the office," he explained. He couldn't verify that her friend had reached her destination.

"Where are my attackers?"

"One fled on foot, and the other is incapacitated. There could be a third one who will help them evade authorities." Julian made a quick call to the police. Disconnecting, he said, "Your friend made it to the office, because several units are already en route. We've been instructed to remain here until they say it's safe to come out."

Chest heaving, she started to sit up.

"Whoa, steady." He moved to assist her, retracting his hand when she hissed in pain. "What's wrong with your shoulder?"

Easing to a sitting position, she rested her head against the wall and balanced herself with both palms on the floor. "I got in the way of a barbell."

Julian shifted closer and lifted her sleeve. The flesh was a mass of dark purple. Concealing a burst of anger, he said evenly, "You'll need to get that examined."

She gingerly rotated her shoulder and raised her arm up and down. "Doesn't feel broken."

"Still, I'm calling for an ambulance." He took out his cell.

"No." Her fingers closed over his wrist. "I'm not going to the hospital."

The entreaty in her eyes was at odds with the militant angle of her chin.

"After what you've endured, you need to be evaluated by a physician. At the very least, you'll need X-rays of that arm and shoulder."

Her fingertips pressed into his pulse point. "This is

personal, Julian. *I* want to decide who knows and who doesn't. If I go there for treatment, every employee will be talking about it."

A shiver ripped through her, and he noticed how cold her fingers were. Tucking away his cell, he covered her fingers with his hand and tried to warm them.

"I can take you to Wilmington."

"I'm fine." She studied his face and sighed. "If it'll make you feel better, I'll call Lincoln. He's a surgeon and good friend."

Julian refused to give voice to curiosity. Whether or not she had a boyfriend was none of his business. "Call him."

"I'll ask him to come to my apartment."

"Make it my apartment."

The protest brewing on her lips died a quick death. "I can't stay in mine, can I?"

"Not anytime soon. You're welcome to my guest bedroom as long as you need it."

Her mouth twisted. "That would mean dragging you deeper into this. Putting you in harm's way. I'll go to a hotel—"

"I'm already in this with you." The thought of Audrey facing these monsters alone was untenable. "I've thwarted the enemy's plans. I've wounded two of their own. My name's on the hit list along with yours."

"I'm so sorry," she whispered. "You did that for me."

"I'd do it again if it meant saving you."

SIX

"Apply this antibiotic ointment a couple of times a day, and baby that shoulder. You're going to be sore for a while."

Audrey scooted off the guest-room desk in Julian's apartment they'd used as a makeshift exam table. "Thanks for coming, Lincoln. I know house calls aren't in your job description."

"Anything to help a friend." He handed her the ointment tube and returned the extra gauze to his backpack-turned-doctor's-bag.

In his late thirties and divorced, Dr. Lincoln Fitzgerald was admired for both his professional skills and charisma. With his smooth olive skin, startling blue eyes and raven hair threaded with silver, he reminded Audrey of a famous Greek tycoon who was often in the news. No wonder Chasity had fallen hard for him.

"Chasity's on call this weekend," he said, "and they needed her to fill a shift. Otherwise, she'd be here demanding answers."

The undisguised concern in his eyes tempted her to recount what had happened. Audrey had admired his humility and commitment to local charities ever since she'd come to work at Onslow General. She'd gotten to know him better since he and Chasity became an item last year. The couple had invited her along on multiple outings, and she'd been treated to lavish meals in his luxurious home. Now she considered him part of her inner circle, which was admittedly quite small.

"The less you know, the better."

"That's hardly a satisfactory answer," he chided. "We're both worried about you, Audrey. We want to help, if we can."

This recent attack flashed through her brain, evoking panic. She'd blacked out, been on the verge of death, only to regain consciousness in Julian's care.

There's no need to be scared, she consoled herself. *Julian's right outside.*

Somehow, he'd become her safe place. Her harbor in the storm.

She had a feeling he'd run far and fast if he knew.

Lincoln slung the backpack over one shoulder and jerked his thumb toward the closed door. "Who's the guard dog?"

Out in the central living area, a television program couldn't mask the almost constant movement of her host. She could picture him prowling around like a caged jungle cat—all sleek muscle, lethal cunning and harnessed power.

"He works with my dad." A simple definition for a man who'd gone to great lengths to save her life. Twice.

"His name sounds familiar."

"Julian is the only survivor of the recent training mishap at Camp Lejeune. You were on vacation at the time, but you might've seen his picture in the local papers."

Understanding dawned. "I remember reading about the helicopter that went down." His brows descended. "Is he the reason for your current troubles?"

"No, not at all."

"You trust him, though?"

Audrey recognized the implication and the telltale hurt. Laying a hand on his sleeve, she said, "He's involved in this through no fault of his own. I can't intentionally put you and Chasity in harm's way."

His phone buzzed, and he looked at the screen. "It's her. She wants an update on your condition."

"Tell her I'm fine."

His gaze narrowed. "*Fine* isn't a word I'd use to describe your current state."

"Lincoln."

"I'll be intentionally evasive. How's that?"

While he typed out a response, Audrey opened the door and almost collided with Julian's wide chest. He steadied her, his fingers gentle on her cool, sensitive skin.

His golden brown gaze scanned her from head to toe before zeroing in on Lincoln. Maybe she was imagining the flare of dislike. Everyone who met Lincoln liked him. Well, except for his ex-wife.

His fingers trailed down her biceps, past her elbow and along her forearm before falling away. The touch was fleeting and insignificant, she was certain, but she felt the effects all the way down to her toes. How she could think about her reaction to him at a time like this was beyond her.

"What's the prognosis?" he asked the surgeon.

"I'm fine," she answered for him. Julian's scent teased her closer, as did his molded shoulders and strong arms.

Forget it, she scolded herself. There was no need to seek solace in his embrace. She'd dealt with Seth's death and the ensuing grief on her own. She'd handle this new trial, too.

Skirting around him, she went into the living room and chose one of the bar stools. Julian had been busy. While she'd been getting examined, he'd laid out a variety of snacks—a bowl of oranges and kiwis, individual trail-mix packets, yogurts and string cheese. She snagged some cheese and peeled open the wrapper.

Breakfast had been an apple, and there hadn't been time for lunch. The police had interviewed her and Julian at length and hadn't released them from the crime scene until every last surface had been swept for prints and DNA samples. Remembering the goon's expression as he'd watched her struggle, she lost her appetite and barely managed to swallow the last bite.

A cold soda can was pressed into her hand. Startled, she glanced up and saw understanding in Julian's face.

"Thanks."

"You'll need to eat more than that to keep up your strength."

Lincoln entered from the bedroom. "She'll require rest, as well."

"I'll rest today," she responded. "Then I'll be back on shift tomorrow."

Julian frowned. Lincoln shook his head. "I'll speak to Veronica and arrange for sick leave."

She popped up. "You will do no such thing." Both men stared at her as if she had two heads. "I can't miss work. I have bills to pay." Her meager savings were for routine emergencies, like a broken-down car or hefty medical bills.

Julian leaned against the end of the bar and crossed his arms. "Staying away from the hospital is the wise move."

Lincoln, along with the rest of the surgical unit, knew about the storage-room attack. He didn't know details, however. "He's right."

"This isn't just about a paycheck. This is about providing adequate patient care. Lincoln, you know we're straining every day simply to have enough staff to run the unit. It's dangerous and unethical. If you want to help, put pressure on HR to fill the vacant positions."

Before Lincoln could reply, Julian cut him off. "We could ask Jacksonville PD if they'll station one or two of their men outside your unit. Hospital security would be on the floor. And I'll be there, as well."

"You're supposed to be recuperating," she admonished, wrapping her palms around the chilled aluminum can.

"Sitting there and doing nothing is the same as sitting here and doing nothing."

"I don't like it." Lincoln looked disgruntled, a rare mood for him. "Too risky."

"I can ask Veronica to shadow me. At the first sign of suspicious activity, I'll clock out and take a leave of absence."

"What about your shoulder? I don't advise lifting anything above five pounds."

"Maybe Veronica or another nurse can pitch in."

When he'd conceded to her wishes and bid them both goodbye, she turned to Julian.

"Why did you take my side?"

His tanned fingers ran lightly over his bandaged wrist and hand. "Because I know what it's like to be banned from doing what you were born to do."

The veneer cracked, allowing her a glimpse of deep-seated anxiety. His future with force recon—and the Marine Corps as a whole—was in jeopardy. She blinked, and the moment passed. He was the implacable, competent marine once more. Untouched by normal human emotion.

Behind the controlled mask, he had to be wrestling with intense grief and misplaced guilt. Audrey was well-acquainted with both. She wanted to help him, to repay him somehow.

She curled her hand around his wrapped palm. "I lost someone close to me. I'm here if you need to talk."

He glanced down at their joined hands. The heat of his skin warmed her through the gauze. His fingers were long and lean, like a piano player's, and his palm was wide and sturdy. She found she didn't want to sever the connection.

This is what happens when you spend too much time alone. You become supersensitive to the simplest of actions.

He gently disengaged. "Thanks for the offer, but I'm good."

It was a lie, but she didn't call him on it.

"Let's talk about what happened at the gym," he said.

"Why?"

"Violent encounters can take a toll if you don't know how to work through them."

Rehashing the evil ordeal was the last thing she wanted right now. "Thanks for the offer, but I'm good," she quipped.

He merely inclined his head. "As you wish."

As he crossed to the desk and rifled through the top drawer, Audrey experienced a pang of regret.

"Julian—"

"What are you in the mood for?" He fanned out a sheaf of pamphlets like playing cards. "Italian? Tex-Mex? Chinese? There's a place on Western Boulevard that rivals my father's cooking. Their dumplings are *'ono.*"

"*'Ono?*"

"Delicious."

Audrey hesitated, wanting to continue the conversation but thinking better of it. Julian had the right idea. They would be spending an indeterminate amount of time together for the foreseeable future. Better to keep matters between them as impersonal as possible.

She pointed to the menu with a dragon printed on the front. "Chinese it is."

* * *

The impenetrable, self-protective shell Julian had cultivated during his years of service wasn't as foolproof as he'd thought. One sincere overture from Audrey, and he'd seriously considered baring his soul. His palm still tingled from her innocent touch. Clenching his fist, he focused on the dull ache while blocking the remembered sadness and appeal in a pair of enchanting blue eyes.

His innate sense of self-preservation warned that Audrey Harris had the power to worm beneath his defenses. If he was ever ready to share his private pain, and he doubted he ever would be, he wouldn't do so with his superior's daughter.

Standing in his kitchen, he looked at the tray he'd prepared and shook his head. A mug of herbal tea joined a turkey sandwich, cereal bar and apple. This was a first—playing host to a woman on the run. Pampering others wasn't his style. Or maybe he hadn't been in the position before. It wasn't because he was infatuated or interested, he reassured himself. Audrey hadn't eaten much of her dinner. Afterward, she'd retreated to the guest bedroom despite giving the impression that she didn't truly wish to be alone.

He paused in the guest room's open doorway. "Mind if I come in?"

Letting the curtains fall into place, she turned. "Of course not."

She'd changed into a pair of worn blue jeans, a black tank top and a thin, zip-up hoodie. The worry and exhaustion cloaking her did nothing to diminish her appeal. There was a vulnerability about her, but also a dogged determination to persevere.

"I brought you a snack," he said, sliding the tray onto the desk. "I'm not used to having anyone stay here besides family. While my sisters aren't shy about raiding the kitchen, I wasn't sure you'd be so comfortable."

Audrey crossed the room to his side, picked up the mug and sniffed. "Smells good."

He shifted to the other side of the desk because her soft, flowing tresses and signature fragrance made him hyperaware of her closeness. "You didn't have much of an appetite earlier, and I don't want you going hungry."

"Thoughtfulness is an admirable quality. Did your parents drill it into you or does it come from growing up with sisters?"

"How am I supposed to answer that without sounding conceited?"

She shrugged. "Tell me about your family," she said, tapping the candid photo pinned to the ribbon-trimmed corkboard above the desk. "How did your parents meet?"

Julian's intention to deliver the food and leave evaporated. He picked up the plate and held it out to her. "I talk. You eat."

A glimmer of humor brightening her eyes, she took a bite of the sandwich.

"My father came to the US to study business and international law. He met my mother, Layla, at university. They married after graduation. I came along that first year. Mom likes to say that she'd planned to return to work, but that I changed her mind."

"Couldn't bear to leave you, huh?"

"I was rather cute as a baby."

She cocked her head. "I'm having trouble imagining you as a cute and cuddly toddler."

Julian was aware he came across as hard-edged and taciturn to some people. For the most part, he gave it little thought. Why it bothered him to think Audrey saw him that way, he had no idea. "My sister Cara was born a year after me. The twins, Emma and Melanie, arrived two years after her."

"Your mom had her hands full."

"She was in her element." He counted himself blessed to have her. Layla's fun-loving, outgoing personality balanced his father's strict, no-nonsense outlook. "She has the ability to make the simplest of activities fun."

"A rare quality."

"Yes."

"What's your father like?"

"Traditional. Studious. He sets high standards for the people in his life." More so for his only son than his daughters, he thought with a trace of bitterness.

"Are you close?"

"Close?" An incredulous laugh burst out. "The only person Chin Tan has allowed to truly know him is my mom."

Her expression clouded. "That must be tough. My dad and I have a good relationship. But then, it's been just the two of us for more than a decade. He's my rock."

"You're fortunate."

"I am. I would've loved to have had my mom around, however." Clearing her throat, she said, "What are your sisters like?"

"Cara is driven to succeed and a whiz in the kitchen. She's parlayed that into a thriving donut business." His mouth watered thinking about her doughy creations. He made a mental note to have a dozen flown in. Pricey, but well worth it. "Emma is more laid-back, like our mom. She's content flipping pancakes at a restaurant she's worked at since her teens. And Melanie is an elementary-school teacher."

"You must miss them."

"They visit me at least once a year, and I take advan-

tage of the free military flights when my schedule allows."
When she'd polished off the sandwich, he opened the cereal bar and handed it to her. "Emma decorated this room without asking for permission," he said, gesturing to the striped comforter and curtains and polka-dot pillows in pink, gold and aqua colors. Flicking the festive paper lei she'd hung on the corner of the corkboard, it suddenly hit him. *"Melia,"* he murmured. *"Pua melia."*

"What's that?"

"I've been trying to place your scent. It's plumeria."

Her brows shot up, and pink infused her cheeks.

"I didn't mean to make you uncomfortable," he said, feeling like an idiot. "I told you my mind is a filing cabinet of useless details. Plumeria reminds me of home. They're used to make leis."

"I don't wear perfume, but I do splurge on hand-milled soap from a locally owned boutique. Chasity took me there. She's one of their favorite customers."

"Chasity is your coworker?"

"And a good friend. She's also Lincoln's girlfriend. You haven't met her yet, but she was there when you were brought into post-op."

The reminder was a timely one. He'd let himself become distracted by his unexpected guest instead of trying to dig for answers. "I know you aren't eager to rehash what happened today, but ignoring it won't make the danger any less real. Those goons aren't your average drug pushers."

Threading her fingers through her hair, she turned away. "I know."

"I'm sure you've heard that sometimes crimes are perpetrated by someone close to the victim."

She whirled back and spread her hands wide. "Like I told the police, I have no idea who's behind this. I don't know who stole the drugs or my log-in. I don't know who administered that dose of epinephrine or why. I can't tell you who in my unit has acted suspicious because *no one* has."

Julian opened a side drawer of the desk and withdrew a pad of paper. "How about we make a list of everyone you come into contact with at the hospital?"

"I may not be chummy with every single one of my coworkers, but I trust them to do right by our patients and by me."

Julian understood how difficult this was for her. Audrey didn't want to believe anyone at Onslow General was capable of such horrible crimes. But if this exercise led to answers, it was worth it.

"Once we're finished, I'll give you control of the TV remote."

Audrey reluctantly accepted the paper. "I'm going to choose a romance."

"I'm asking you to do something unpleasant," he said somberly. "It's only fair you demand the same of me."

SEVEN

"What do you mean I'm not allowed to work?"

Audrey's voice rose in pitch, drawing curious, darting glances from medical personnel and visitors traversing the lobby's intersecting corridors. She'd counted on work as a way to distract herself from everything going on in her life. Helping patients would, in turn, help her.

The hospital president regarded Audrey with a long-suffering air. "We appreciate your devotion to your patients, Miss Harris, but you must understand that allowing you to continue is out of the question."

"Local law enforcement will be on the floor, in addition to our own security members." Tugging on her ID, she glanced toward the entrance. Julian was on the move, pacing back and forth and giving everyone a once-over. He'd be there in an unofficial capacity, but she wasn't about to mention that.

Harper's associate, an icy blonde wearing a no-nonsense pantsuit, spoke up. "This has the potential to be a legal nightmare." Her eyes glittered with cold professionalism. "You should know we've started an internal investigation. Can we count on your cooperation?"

Audrey swallowed hard. "Of course."

"Good." She extended her hand. "We'll need your ID badge until the matter is closed."

Humiliation burned in her cheeks. She was grateful Julian wasn't close enough to witness this conversation. Without a word, she removed the chain and dropped it into the blonde's grip.

"You have my number and email," she said, trying to hold it together. "I'll expect to hear from you."

Harper cast a sideways glance at the blonde before speaking. "Miss Harris, this really is for your own good."

With a terse nod, Audrey pivoted and started for the bank of glass doors at a furious pace. Julian caught up to her just as she exited the building.

"Where are you going?"

"Anywhere but here."

"What happened?"

"I'm not welcome at the hospital until they get answers," she muttered, fighting angry tears.

She was essentially being punished for something beyond her control. When they reached his black Mustang, she stopped short. "Julian, what if these people plant evidence? They've already tried to pin the patient mishaps on me. I—I could go to jail."

With a quick survey of the parking lot, he opened the passenger door. "This has escalated beyond a simple frame job. They aim to silence you for good."

Audrey slid into the low-slung seat, defeat weighing on her. "Don't bother sugarcoating it," she said with a pinch of sarcasm.

Julian's intense gaze met hers. "That's not really what you want, is it?"

Groaning, she let her head drop against the seat. "No."

He shut the door and strode around the car's front. Settling behind the wheel, he started the engine but didn't put it in Reverse. "While your desire to support your coworkers and patients is admirable, the risks are undeniable. The hospital's decision isn't about your innocence or guilt. It's about protecting themselves."

If anything, his words made her feel worse. "I'm not totally selfless, you know. I need the demands of a grueling shift to stay sane. No time to ponder my problems. Just assess and react."

Twelve blissful hours of escape.

He lifted one shoulder. "You're human."

She stared out the tinted window and contemplated what they would do to fill the hours. Last night, she'd been too exhausted to dwell on her predicament. Julian's long-suffering expressions and wry quips during the movie had struck her as comical. Despite everything, she'd actually enjoyed the evening. He was a good guy. Patient and thoughtful. Not once had he made her feel like a burden.

Out on the main road, Julian did frequent checks of the rearview and side mirrors. "We should forward that list of names to the police department."

Audrey didn't immediately comment. That list consisted of strangers, acquaintances and friends. Casting suspicion on anyone she cared about did not sit well with her.

"How deep into their lives will the detectives go?" she said, watching the various businesses flash past.

"I get that you're worried about inconveniencing your friends. To be honest, they'll fall under law enforcement's scrutiny with or without your input. The hospital's, too. The list ensures the detectives don't overlook anyone."

"I suppose."

"Hey." His fingers skimmed her knuckles, drawing her gaze to him. "Don't blame yourself. You did what was right. It took courage to report the thefts."

Admiration shone in his eyes, making her heart swell.

"It's time to loop in your father, Audrey."

The giddiness faded.

"You don't want him learning about it from someone else."

"You're right." At his raised brows, she said, "This is

too big to contain. He has too many friends at the hospital."

"It's Saturday. Is he home? I can drive you over."

"I'll tell him tomorrow. I need time to rehearse my delivery method."

"Understood." He was pulling into the apartment complex when Audrey's phone beeped. Retrieving it from her backpack, she saw Chasity's name on the screen. She read the text several times.

He killed the engine. "You look conflicted."

"Lincoln and Chasity are hosting a dinner party tonight. I completely forgot about it."

"Time?"

"Six o'clock. I promised to go, but that was before…" She trailed off. "Chas insisted I ask you to accompany me."

"Do you want to go?"

"Keeping busy seems like a good idea right now, but you're not being paid to be my bodyguard."

"Lincoln strikes me as the kind of guy who'd live in a gated community."

"How did you guess?"

"He's a surgeon who wears three-hundred-dollar loafers and a Citizen's watch worth several grand. Even his backpack has a designer label. The man puts stock in value and luxury."

"You're good. However, I know for a fact that watch was a gift from his ex-wife, Gina. Chas would prefer he get rid of it. He and Chasity like to shop, but they don't pay top dollar. They search for bargains. Those loafers were probably half-price."

"What can I say? Reading people is an art, not a science."

"I don't want to know what you've assumed about me."

His full, sculpted mouth curved in a mischievous grin. Audrey's pulse raced in response.

"Well, I—"

She put her fingers on his lips to stop him. "Really. I don't want to know."

Awareness flared to life in his eyes, and he curled his fingers around hers. Time seemed to slow. For the first time since Seth's death, Audrey yearned to feel a connection with another man. She was attracted to Julian. What woman wouldn't be? He was handsome and strong, confident and capable.

But she wasn't ready. And he wasn't interested, because he released her and turned away. "Where does Lincoln live?"

Rubbing her palm across her scrub pants, she named a waterfront neighborhood that took advantage of the river view.

"I know it," he said. "The gates will prove a deterrent for any unsavory types. Tell Chasity to expect us."

"You won't know anyone there," she warned. "Most of the invited guests are hospital employees."

"Bingo."

"You plan to treat this like a mission. You're going to try and ferret out information that could shed light on the case."

"It's a long shot, but worth a try."

"I'll do what I can to help you. This has to end before anyone else gets hurt."

The gate-hut employee emerged to peruse Julian's driver's license. "You're both on the list, Sergeant Tan," he said. "Have a good evening."

He rolled up the window. "Which way?"

Audrey gave him directions, hoping her nervousness

wasn't showing. The gate lamps bathed Julian in filmy light. He'd taken her breath away when he'd emerged from his bedroom in a well-cut black suit, complete with immaculate white shirt and patterned silk tie. Seated close to him in the snug confines of the Mustang, she was attuned to his every move. His cologne was subtle and refreshing. One hand held the steering wheel, and the injured one rested on his thigh. Those hands had defended her and rescued her.

"You still want to do this?" His deep, smooth voice washed over her. "Because we can ditch the party and have pizza at home, if you'd rather. I'll even let you pick the toppings."

"Tempting offer. I'll take a rain check."

While she wasn't excited to endure the curious stares and outright questions she'd no doubt receive, she hoped something good would come of it. Julian was one of the best. She had that on good authority—her dad didn't brag on just anyone. If anyone could tease out information that would lead to answers, it was him.

Lincoln's home was situated at the end of a cul-de-sac. Built to resemble an Italian villa, the sprawling house boasted a brick driveway leading to a side portico and a three-car garage. Lush, manicured lawns were edged with sculpted hedges and flowers that had bloomed early due to the unseasonal heat. A high stucco wall blocked the view of the rear property, which she knew consisted of a kidney-shaped pool, outdoor kitchen and dining area and sweeping lawns that sloped to a well-maintained dock.

The stucco exterior gleamed like polished pearl in the waning sunlight.

Julian whistled. "Nice digs."

"Wait until you see the interior."

Julian found a convenient parking spot on the street.

He assisted her out of the vehicle, his hand resting against her back as they made their way along the sidewalk. His touch set off mini fireworks in her middle. He exuded a protective air that Audrey wasn't accustomed to. For much of her and Seth's relationship, she'd had to be the strong one, the nurturer.

At the carved wooden doors, he performed a quick visual examination of her. "You look beautiful, Audrey."

The doors swung open. Chasity, radiant in a blue cocktail dress that showed off her trim figure, greeted them with an enthusiastic smile. "Right on time." She gave Audrey a partial hug to avoid her bruised shoulder. "I'm glad you decided to come. Lincoln gave me a report on your condition, but he was frustratingly short on details. You and I are going to have a chat later."

The glint in her eyes rivaled the twin diamonds in her ears. Chasity's petite form and fair beauty masked a backbone of steel. Audrey would have to work hard to keep her friend from learning of the recent horror she'd endured.

"The last time I saw you," Chasity said to Julian, "you were in rough shape. I'm happy to meet you in better circumstances."

"I'm grateful Audrey was in the right place at the right time," he said.

"You couldn't have asked for a better nurse. As far as I'm concerned, she's one of the top RNs in the hospital." Tucking a stray curl behind her ear, she addressed Audrey. "Harper had better let you come back soon."

Catching sight of a new, significant piece of jewelry, all thoughts of her banishment vanished.

"You're engaged?" Bringing her friend's hand closer, she admired the exquisite pear-shaped diamond. "When did this happen? Why didn't you tell me?"

A blush suffused her cheeks. "Last night. Apparently,

he bought the ring weeks ago and was planning an elaborate proposal dinner. Something changed his mind, because he sprung it on me after my shift while I was still in my soiled scrubs."

"I'm happy for you, Chas. You and Lincoln are a great match."

"I didn't think he'd be ready for marriage anytime soon, considering how Gina treated him. I'll be putting my house up for sale later this month."

"Congratulations to you both," Julian inserted. "When's the big day?"

"We haven't set a date yet, but we've decided on an intimate ceremony. Will you come dress-shopping with me, Audrey?"

"You seriously have to ask? Of course I will. Anytime."

Julian shifted beside her, a cautionary look in his eyes. She wasn't exactly free to make plans, was she?

Chasity seemed oblivious to the silent exchange. "What am I thinking, keeping you out here on the stoop? Come in." She ushered them into the high-ceilinged foyer. Classical music mingled with clinking glasses and conversation. "Dinner is in an hour. There are appetizers set out in the living area to tide you over."

Audrey caught a glimpse of herself and Julian in the gilt mirror. How normal they looked, she mused. No one would guess that they'd been brushed by violence.

Her shell-pink cardigan, worn over a silky, sleeveless blouse of the same hue, covered the ugly bruising that marred her shoulder. The scarf hid her throat, as did her hair, which fell past her shoulders in tumbling waves. Julian's compliment had surprised and thrilled her.

Brushing lint from her snug black pants, she walked with him to the archway leading to the tiled living area with windows overlooking the pool and, in the distance, the navy blue waters of the river. Audrey recognized most of the guests. One, in particular, caused her to startle.

Chasity noticed. "Veronica overheard me talking about tonight and hinted that she had nothing to do. I had to invite her."

"I'm surprised she'd angle for an invitation," she murmured. Veronica stood on the outer edge of a group comprised of nurses and surgical residents. "She doesn't usually socialize with work peers."

"Maybe she was feeling lonely."

"Is that Heather talking to David?" Audrey couldn't understand the X-ray tech's appeal. He gave her the creeps.

"They arrived together. Heather must've mustered her courage. Or maybe David recognized her interest and acted." Chasity's attention was diverted to one of two doorways to the kitchen, where a uniformed young man waited. "I have to oversee the kitchen staff. The catering company we chose is a new one, and they are second-guessing every decision." Giving Audrey's hand a squeeze, she said, "I'll catch up with you later. Go. Mingle. Try and enjoy yourself."

When Chasity had gone, Julian led Audrey to the nearest appetizer station, where food was spread out on an ornate buffet server. Positioned a few steps from where they'd entered, it provided an unobstructed view of the room.

"Sparkling water?"

His fingers brushed hers as she accepted the proffered bottle.

"What do you know about Veronica?" He perused the offerings, his back to the crowd, and appeared as if he didn't have a care in the world.

"Very little. I've heard tidbits here and there. If they are to be believed, she married her high-school sweetheart right after graduation, only to lose him a year later in a car accident." She took a sip of the bubbly, lemon-flavored water. "Her second marriage ended in divorce a decade ago."

"Kids?" He popped a shrimp concoction in his mouth.

"None."

Swallowing, he pointed to the tray. "You should try one."

"No, thanks." She was too worked up to eat.

"So, as far as you know, she's single. It's possible she receives spousal support. I'm not familiar with North Carolina's divorce laws." Turning, he scanned the crowd. "Has she given any clues she might be in trouble financially?"

"She doesn't share that sort of information."

"Her clothes aren't designer-label. Costume jewelry. Of course, she could be taking pains to hide financial gain. What sort of vehicle does she drive?"

"I've never paid attention."

He took a long draw from the bottle and inclined his head. "Let's make our way over there without being obvious about it."

"As a first-time visitor," she said, playing along, "you'll want to see the view."

Approval lit his eyes. "Absolutely."

On their way to the oversize windows, several people spoke to Audrey, causing her to have to pause and introduce Julian. They commiserated with her over her obligatory leave of absence, but their true focus was on her date. She'd been so focused on tonight's goal that she hadn't thought about the conjecture they'd arouse.

When they finally reached a spot with an uninhibited view of the river, Julian acted suitably impressed, commenting on the grounds and boats bobbing in the water. As dusk descended, lights began to twinkle on the horizon.

"You don't make a habit of bringing dates around, do you?"

She cast a quick glance at his profile. "What makes you say that?"

"Easy," another voice quipped. "Everyone knows Audrey still pines for her lost fiancé."

They twisted around to face Veronica, who'd abandoned the other group. Her makeup looked slightly less garish paired with regular clothes. "The fact that she's in public with a man other than her dad is headline news."

Julian wrapped his arm around her waist and tucked her against his side. "Then I count myself a fortunate man."

Veronica's upper lip curled. "It's a bit too poetic for me." Her bloodshot gaze bounced between them. "Dating the nurse who saved your life."

"Really? I think it's romantic." He smiled down at Audrey. The full force of that suave smile and accompanying warmth in his eyes made her weak in the knees. She liked being close to him. Liked the feeling, however fleeting, of being part of a couple.

It's fake. A show.

Julian wasn't her date.

"Romance is for lonely, weak people."

"Then there must be a lot of lonely, weak people in the world," retorted Audrey.

Julian's hand navigated up her back and, settling warm and heavy on her neck, gave a gentle, warning squeeze.

Outwardly, he made a commiserating sound. "You're married to your work, then?"

Veronica shrugged and her gaze pierced Audrey. "When you're young and fresh, the job seems exciting and noble. After a while, it loses its sparkle. I had envisioned retiring early, but that's out now."

"I'm sorry to hear that," he said. "Did you have plans to travel?"

"Hardly. I was going to move to Sarasota." A loud crash in the kitchen distracted her. "Sounds like dinner might be delayed. I'm starving. Who eats this late, anyway?"

With a parting word, she marched to the buffet server and began to fill a small plate.

Julian's arm fell away, and it took several seconds for Audrey to respond in kind. It felt natural to lean against him. Her cheeks flamed. He was insightful. Had he noticed she *liked* being close to him?

"What's the reason she can't retire?" she asked to cover her embarrassment.

"And what's in Sarasota? We need to do some digging into her life, see if there's sufficient motivation for her to dabble in the narcotic industry."

He threaded his fingers through hers. "Do you mind the show of affection? I thought it would give them something other than the recent mishaps to gossip about."

Could he truly not detect her increased heart rate? See the blush on her cheeks?

"I don't mind," she said, her voice husky. "It's a means to an end."

"Good." He nodded, his eyes holding her captive. A girl could get lost in those eyes. "Why don't you introduce me to more people? There's a chance the person who's using you to cover up their criminal activity is in this room."

Reconnaissance was an inherent part of his job. Working with a partner was also commonplace. Pretending to be a beautiful nurse's date? Out of his comfort zone. Audrey wasn't just any civilian, either. Julian had no doubt Trent Harris would run him through the ringer if he knew what they were up to.

He glanced at his watch. One hour in, and he'd met and dismissed ninety-five percent of the guests. While Veronica was a disgruntled character, he wasn't fully convinced she was funneling narcotics out of Onslow General.

A frown tugged Audrey's brows together. "Lincoln and Chasity don't look pleased."

From their vantage point beside one of three gleaming leather sofas, they had an unobstructed view into the well-equipped kitchen. The hired staff bounced from counter to counter, bumping into one another in their haste. The couple stood off to the side, observing the chaos and conversing with each other.

"The guests don't seem to mind the delay," he said.

"I'm afraid coming here was a pointless exercise."

"It's too early to call it a bust. We're identifying possible players."

"Everyone here acts like normal, law-abiding citizens."

He got her frustration. "The key word is *acts*. You wouldn't believe how many different faces evil assumes."

She readjusted the scarf again. The slight tremor in her hand had him questioning if bringing her here was the right thing, so soon after the attempts on her life. She hadn't complained of fatigue or distress, but the signs were there. Shadows beneath her eyes. Fatigue bracketing her mouth.

"Let's skip out early," he said, smoothing an errant strand behind her ear.

Her eyes widened. Because of his suggestion or the uncalled-for caress?

"Why?" Her gaze dropped to his arm. "Are you in pain? You're taking the prescribed antibiotics, aren't you?"

"I'm good. I thought you might like peace and quiet, after all."

"I'll stick it out." She gestured to the foyer. "I'm going to the powder room."

"I'll come with you."

She arched an eyebrow in challenge. "Not necessary. It's a few steps from the entrance."

He weighed her desire for privacy against the potential for danger.

"No one is going to attack me in Lincoln's home, especially not in the guest bath."

Since he couldn't be sure of that, he gave her a head start without informing her he planned to follow. When she passed through the archway and ventured left, he discarded his empty water bottle and made to go after her.

But Lincoln waylaid him. "Is Audrey all right? She looks distracted."

That the surgeon cared about Audrey was obvious. According to her, Lincoln had included her instead of regarding her as a third wheel. "She's holding her own."

"She should be at home resting. I told Chasity not to pressure her into coming tonight. She wanted her here for the big announcement." Setting his glass on the end table, he turned to face Julian more fully. "You obviously have some sort of stake in her life. Help her see the importance of taking care of herself. The strain she's been under these past weeks is taking its toll."

The fact that the other man had pegged the situation outright irked Julian. He'd known a couple of Special Forces guys who'd gone on to join the Secret Service. Their number-one rule—don't get emotionally attached to the person under their protection. Surely, he hadn't grown too close to Audrey already.

"I'll talk to her."

"I'd appreciate it. Audrey's special to my soon-to-be wife, which makes her special in my book, as well."

"Chasity relayed the good news. Congratulations."

"Thank you."

Julian gestured to the framed photographs on the end table. "Those your kids?"

A proud smile creased his cheeks. "Theo and Therese."

"How old are they?"

"Theo turned eleven last month. Therese is fourteen."

"Your son is the spitting image of you." The girl, on the other hand, looked nothing like him.

"I hear what you're too polite to ask. Therese is my biological daughter. She happens to take after her mother in every way save for her greedy heart. Therese isn't driven to own the best of everything." He waved a hand to encompass the home. "Before you label me a hypocrite, I would've been content with a simple farmhouse in Richlands," he said, indicating the farming community not far from the Camp Lejeune base. "Gina had to have the upscale life that goes along with my career."

Lincoln's unresolved bitterness toward his ex-wife didn't bode well for his new marriage. Julian wondered if Chasity was oblivious or merely an optimist. And why was Lincoln trying to convince him he wasn't materialistic?

"What's he doing here?" Lincoln scowled at someone behind Julian.

Twisting around, he recognized Frank Russo. "He wasn't invited?"

"Not by us. Chasity isn't a fan."

Veronica separated from the crowd and went to intercept him.

"Perhaps Iron Nurse asked him to come," Lincoln mused.

"Are they friendly outside of work?"

"I couldn't say. Do me a favor, will you? While I'm busy

soothing Chasity's nerves and making sure everyone has enough to eat and drink, keep Russo away from Audrey."

"Is he a threat to her?"

"He was an unhappy man to start with. The staff shortage has been an issue for months. This situation with Audrey has exacerbated the problem. He's been complaining to everyone who'll listen that the excess overtime is damaging his health and threatening his ability to properly care for patients."

The man looked like someone who didn't take proper care of himself. Whether that stemmed from extra hours and stress, Julian wasn't prepared to say. Frank could be drowning his sorrows in alcohol or dabbling in drugs. That wasn't his problem. His problem was that Frank blamed Audrey instead of the hospital. Someone nursing a grudge could potentially put thoughts into action.

Frank's tight gaze punched through the room. Searching for Audrey?

Julian started for the foyer, dodging furniture and guests. She should've returned by now. He told himself she was probably lingering in the powder room, savoring the reprieve from prying eyes and not-so-subtle conjecture.

The grand entryway was vacant. Quickly spotting a closed door in the adjacent hallway, he approached and knocked.

"Audrey?"

He twisted the knob. The door swung inward, revealing a nicely appointed half bath. No Audrey. And there wasn't a window, meaning no one could've breached the space.

He emerged into the hallway, his gut a knot of apprehension.

Where was she?

EIGHT

"Go past the home office and guest bedrooms. The master suite is at the end of this corridor."

Audrey thanked the young staffer who'd informed her the guest bath was unusable and directed her to the master bath. She'd been in Lincoln's home plenty of times, but she hadn't ventured into his personal space.

The girl hustled back to her duties, and Audrey entered an airy, yet masculine bedroom. Airy thanks to tall windows and the high ceiling that was crisscrossed with beams, and masculine due to the heavy, carved furniture pieces and dark color palette. Feeling like an intruder, she hurried to the bathroom, not pausing to investigate the patio visible through the double doors.

She locked the door and, using one of the available hand towels, dampened and folded it into a rectangle. Removing her scarf, she perched on the soaking tub's edge and pressed the cool cloth to her forehead.

Julian would come looking for her if she didn't return soon. She needed five minutes to regroup. The party had been a bad idea. Everything that had happened—the patient incidents, the break-in, the attempts on Julian's life and hers—had started to press in, making her heart throb and her throat constrict. She'd never had a panic attack before, but she knew the signs. It had felt as if everyone in the room was watching her. Either to gauge her demeanor after being barred from the hospital, or to decide if she'd finally braved the waters of the dating world.

Veronica's comment about Seth, combined with Audrey's reaction to Julian's touch, had her battling a curious mix of guilt, regret and defensiveness.

I'm weak, God. I'm not as strong as I pretend to be. Please let this end.

Audrey didn't understand why He was allowing her to walk through these troubles, but she trusted Him to walk beside her. Guide her. Protect her. He'd provided the best possible guardian, hadn't He? Julian's presence in her life presented its own unique challenges, but she was grateful all the same.

The handle turned before the door vibrated with a firm knock. "Hello?"

While the thick wood masked the voice's timbre, she could tell it was a man speaking. Julian.

"Coming."

She placed the towel into a hamper, grabbed her scarf, unlocked the door and jerked it open. "I'm sorry, I—"

The tall, lanky man in front of her was not Julian. His outfit let her know he was part of the catering staff.

"Oh, I thought you were someone else."

He didn't speak. Chasity wouldn't like his rudeness or the fact he hadn't restrained his shoulder-length hair. Audrey moved to pass him. When he remained in place, uneasiness skittered along her spine. A split second later, he lunged for her. One arm came around her upper body like a vise, imprisoning her arms. Her hurt shoulder spasmed. His hand clamped over her mouth. Her scream was muffled. No one would hear her cries if she didn't act fast.

She kicked out. Stomped his feet. Fought his grip.

He grunted but didn't loosen his hold.

The patio doors flew open, and in strode two more men—identical twins of terror. They converged on her. Within a matter of seconds, they'd bound her ankles and wrists with rope and gagged her. No words were spoken.

Their eyes were blank caverns, their features stark. Expert kidnappers and killers.

Julian, where are you?

Audrey squirmed and moaned, hoping the noise was enough to alert someone. Anyone.

The long-haired one produced a cloud of black material. As he came toward her, his intent became clear.

He was going to put that over her head. She wouldn't be able to see what was happening or anticipate what was coming.

Panic clawed at her insides. She strained to free herself from the other two holding her up. Their strong fingers dug into her flesh. The black material whispered over her hair, then her face and neck.

She felt herself being lifted and carried outside. The sensation of being suspended above the earth, raised high and low and passed between rough pairs of hands, was the stuff of nightmares. Terrified, she screamed against the gag. Over and over again until her throat became raw.

When she was tossed like a laundry sack onto an unforgiving metal surface, she fell silent. What now? Where was she? Where were they taking her?

Movement registered beside her. A shoe jolted her hip, and she flinched.

The sound of doors slamming was followed by the sensation of darkness. An engine rumbled to life. The floor beneath her jerked, and she rolled, slamming her head against jutting metal. Lightning arcs radiated through her skull.

The movement continued, and she realized she was in a vehicle.

Her attackers had her in their grasp.

Julian wasn't going to reach her in time.

* * *

Julian went from room to room searching for Audrey. He'd tried her cell. It had gone straight to voice mail. With each passing minute, the certainty that trouble had found her solidified in his gut.

He entered the room at the end of the corridor and charged over to the bed, where her scarf was lying on the floor. The bed comforter was rumpled, and a decorative pillow had fallen between the bedside table and mattress.

"Audrey? You in here?"

The bathroom yielded not a single clue. Out in the room again, he noticed a set of patio doors tucked into a corner alcove. He turned off the bedroom light, readied his weapon and stole into the cool night. What sounded like commands spoken in a foreign language drifted to him.

Julian started to investigate, only to stop when his shoe connected with something. The object skittered across the painted cement and landed in the mulch. He quickly realized it was a cell phone. The screen responded to his actions, showing badly cracked glass and a background photograph of a younger Audrey with who he assumed were nursing students.

Her smiling face leaped out at him. She looked happier than he'd ever seen her. Radiant and carefree, before danger became her stalker.

His stomach went into free fall.

Audrey had counted on him to keep her safe.

Pocketing her phone, he sprinted past thick shrubbery hugging the foundation and onto a wide swath of grass between the house and a high stucco privacy wall. A half moon aided the grounds' lamps in combating the darkness. Scaling the wall took more effort than usual, thanks to weeks of forced inactivity. He landed on the brick-paved driveway just as a white catering van left the portico and rolled onto the street. Its lights were off.

They had Audrey, and if he let that van out of his sight, she'd be lost forever.

Blanking his mind to everything but his mission, Julian raced across the lawn, careful to avoid the lights on the grounds. They couldn't know they'd been seen.

These were her final hours.

Audrey implored God to grant her divine peace and acceptance. Her burning drive to survive wasn't showing signs of wavering, however. She had too much left to do and experience. With her life in jeopardy, she realized she wanted to love again. To be loved. She wanted to be brave, like Julian. Her bodyguard had dominated her thoughts during the interminable ride.

He'd sink deeper into self-blame because of this. He'd assume responsibility for whatever happened to her, and she hated that. If she could get a message to him, she'd tell him that he'd been her rock during the most harrowing time of her life.

Another thought struck her. When her dad learned of Julian's role, he'd blame him, too. In his anger and grief, there was no telling what he'd do.

She had to get free, but how?

The restraining ropes were so tight, her feet were slowly going numb. Her wrists ached and her bruised and battered shoulder protested the awkward position. She'd have to wait until they reached their destination and pray an opportunity presented itself.

Dread pounded behind her eyes. She'd faced this enemy twice and would've succumbed to their attacks, if not for Julian's interference. He'd been her faithful rescuer. This time, she was on her own.

The man riding with her hadn't spoken a word, so when his guttural voice shattered the silence, she recoiled. He wasn't talking to her, she realized, as unfamiliar speech echoed off the thin walls. He must be speaking into a phone or radio.

The vehicle slowed, and Audrey's heart rate tripled. Would she have a chance? Would a window of escape present itself? Or would the end be quick and hopefully painless?

Her ruminations abruptly ceased as the vehicle stopped and she heard the doors yanked open. Fresh air washed over her. She shivered. The temperature had dropped in the sun's absence.

Hands seized her feet and yanked, sliding her along the cold, ridged metal floor of the vehicle. She yelped but didn't resist. Had to bide her time. Let them think she would passively go along with their plan.

Adrenaline flooded her body to the point that she trembled with the need to expend it. The strangers carried her through the night, one at her feet and the other at her shoulders. Her ears strained to catch clues that might aid her. She thought she heard a boat horn in the distance. They were near the river or the ocean.

Their dress shoes skimmed the ground, catching stray gravel from time to time. Doors opened and closed, and she sensed the change immediately. They were inside a building with a humid interior that smelled of moss and foliage.

Audrey was placed on soft, smooth cushions. Disoriented, she battled rising panic and nausea.

"Is this how we treat invited guests, gentlemen?"

The black covering was removed, and she was maneuvered into a sitting position. A silver-haired man in a pinstripe suit occupied one of several wood-and-leather chairs arranged around an animal-print rug and abstract wooden coffee table. When his shrewd, gunmetal eyes completed a thorough inspection of her, he lifted a single finger.

"Remove the gag."

His voice held a trace of an accent, but she couldn't place it. Three men flanked the leather sofa, the same ones who'd bound and gagged her in Lincoln's bedroom. The long-haired one obeyed the command. The twins scowled at her.

She did a surreptitious survey of her surroundings, desperate for a way out. They'd brought her to a warehouse, but it didn't seem to be the average storage or working space. Shadows draped the cavernous interior. Unusual sounds penetrated the stillness—trickling water and crickets chirruping.

After her gag was removed, Audrey worked her jaw to relieve the stiffness. When she didn't speak, the silver-haired man's eyebrows lifted and humor touched his lips.

"You have nothing to say, Miss Harris?"

"What do you want with me?" Her voice had a smoky rasp to it.

"Bring the lady some water," he ordered. "Untie her."

His henchmen sprang into action, slicing the ropes and presenting her with a cold bottle. She didn't dare drink it.

"I do apologize for the drama." His smile was almost benevolent. "But then, you've proven to be more of a challenge than we anticipated."

"Because I didn't die when it was convenient for you?"

He chuckled. "I'll admit to my mistake. I should not have ordered your death before exploring all the possibilities."

"Who are you?"

"These men call me Boss. My enemies have given me the moniker Jungle King. To you, I'm simply Gerald."

A man who employed myriad henchmen and who'd accrued enemies had to be involved in organized crime. But what would he want with the relatively small amount of narcotics he managed to steal from the hospital? It wasn't enough to turn a huge profit.

A high-pitched shriek assaulted her eardrums. Seeing her cringe, Gerald gave a dismissive wave of his fingers.

"That's probably Brutus. I've brought several of my macaws with me this trip. He's unhappy with his temporary accommodations."

"Why am I here?"

"I'd like to offer you an opportunity for lucrative employment."

Audrey gaped at him. "First you want me dead. Now you're offering me a job?"

"I understand your confusion. I will explain everything. But first, let me give you a tour of my home away from home." Standing, he held out his hand. A gold-and-emerald ring flashed, and gold cuff links at his wrists resembled wild birds, wings outstretched and beaks open.

She had no desire to take the hand of the man who'd orchestrated her nightmare. Ignoring the discomfort in her extremities, she pushed off the couch and stood on her own. His mouth thinned, but his gaze remained upbeat.

Gerald sent the men another signal. Lights flickered on, illuminating a cavernous space that left Audrey speechless.

"What is this?"

He strolled toward a massive aquarium stocked with gray, reflective fish. "My permanent residence is in the Amazon jungle. While not my birth country, Brazil has become my favorite spot on earth." He trailed his fingers along the glass. "Business often calls me away. I've gone to great lengths to bring part of the jungle with me."

"Those are piranhas?"

His smile, and the flash of angular, white teeth, unnerved her.

"Careful, Miss Harris. Don't dip your hand in."

As he led her through a maze of exhibits, Audrey felt as if she was in an aquarium. Not the family-friendly kind, either. He took delight in explaining the deadly aspects of his live collection. Bullet ants with bites that felt like gunshot wounds. Giant centipedes—some about a foot long—that also inflicted suffering. Electric eels. Brazilian wandering spiders.

Then there were the snakes—at least a dozen of them, breathtaking and impressive and intimidating. One of the green anacondas weighed over two hundred pounds, he informed her. She worked to conceal her unease. Audrey was beginning to suspect her mysterious captor didn't have these species here for his comfort and pleasure, but rather to intimidate his "guests."

They were deep into the building when a commotion drew her gaze to a series of rooms along the far side, all with metal doors and large, darkened windows. A pair of well-dressed men dragged an unconscious man from one of the rooms by his arms. Raised welts distorted his arms and legs.

Gerald's forehead creased with displeasure. Taking her arm, he turned her back to the poison-dart-frog exhibit and began to explain their usefulness. She couldn't concentrate. Her mind remained on the victim.

"You use them to torture people who don't bend to your will, don't you?"

He stopped in midsentence, his brows descending. "You're an astute young lady." Drawing in a deep breath, he contemplated the frogs. "Sometimes it becomes necessary to provide incentive, if you will."

"And if those incentives fail?"

He regarded her with an enigmatic gaze. "I'm sure it's challenging for you to understand my methods, given your commitment to helping others." He shrugged. "There are unsavory aspects to my business."

"What business is that, exactly?"

"To make money, Miss Harris. More money than you can imagine. Come, there's more to show you."

She resisted. "My medical knowledge doesn't extend beyond the human body. If you mean to offer me a job caring for your pets—"

"I have a competent caretaker on my payroll." His fingers clamped onto her upper arm, the steel-like grip at odds with his suave demeanor. "You will understand soon enough."

Aware of the goons shadowing their movements, Audrey didn't put up a fight. They knew the layout and placement of the exits. She didn't. They were armed. She wasn't. Even if she managed to take out one—and that was a big *if*—there were at least half a dozen more who'd descend upon her.

Her chances of escape were slim. Hope remained alive solely because the crime boss wanted her for something. Whether or not she would prove useful remained to be seen. She couldn't fathom what he planned to propose she do for him. If she could bring herself to do it, she could buy herself some time. If not…it would surely mean the end for her.

NINE

Julian pocketed the wire cutters he kept in his car trunk and climbed through the opening he'd created. Spiny bushes extended along the fence line, blocking the view of the industrial lot from the main road. He shoved his way between them. Once on the other side, he stopped to formulate a mental map of the enemy's territory.

To his left, a high metal fence topped with barbed wire ran the length of the side road that dead-ended at the river. A paved parking lot stood between him and a boxy, black warehouse that was parallel to the water. Not a single window or door was visible from this angle. A handful of foreign cars occupied spaces close to the building. No sign of the catering van he'd followed here. It had entered through a section of the fence that opened and closed by remote control. A second warehouse sat on his right, the back end adjacent to the fence behind him and the front facing the distant river. It was older, with signs of rust and wear.

Which to investigate first? Every second Audrey was with her captors was life or death.

He hadn't even considered involving local law enforcement. There wasn't time to call in a SWAT team. Plus, they had to play by a certain set of rules. He wasn't bound by oaths or taxpayers' money.

Preaccident, he would've shot off texts to his teammates. They would've descended on the target and worked out an infiltration plan. He was on his own now, and he inwardly railed against their pointless, premature deaths.

He freed his weapon from its holster. Audrey wasn't going to suffer the same tragedy. No way.

Hazy light from streetlamps bounced off the car windows. Their proximity to the black structure cemented his decision. *Please, Lord, let it be the right one.*

He didn't take the time to analyze the unexpected plea to his Creator. Scanning for security cameras, he took a circuitous route, keeping to the trees and then traveling the length of the older warehouse. At the corner, he surveyed the area that had been in his blind spot. He counted seven shipping containers. A sleek, red Ferrari was sandwiched between the containers and identical box trucks. Beyond that, a modest-size yacht was moored to a short dock.

Movement in his peripheral vision registered. Pressing close against the weathered siding, he studied the goon with an M16 slung over his shoulder. That was some serious firepower. He paced beneath an awning while puffing on a cigarette. Behind him, garage doors flanked a set of double doors—Julian's way into that building.

About twenty-five yards stretched between him and the first car. No cover. Nothing to hide his presence.

He'd have to be fast.

Crouching low, he waited for the goon to pivot and retreat in the opposite direction. The instant his shoe sole rotated on the cement, Julian made for the car. He reached it in time, but barely. No way to know if cameras had caught his progress and alerted the building's occupants.

Peering around the bumper, he again waited for his opportunity. He got it when the goon took a long drag of his cigarette and bent to grind it into a receptacle.

Julian sprang into action. The element of surprise gave him an edge.

"Psst."

The guy whirled around. Julian balled his fist and landed a swift, hard punch to his temple. His head snapped to the side, and his knees buckled. He slumped to the ground. Julian crushed his phone and comm device and relieved him of his weapons. If he had the means, he'd truss him up. At least this would slow him down once he regained consciousness.

The double doors had a pass-code lock. If he'd had a drill with him, he could've gotten it open. He had to resort to breaking off the knob with the M16's butt stock, then kicking it in. Inside, he found himself in a long hallway with multiple doors. He would have to work his way through them until he located Audrey. But first, he had to deal with the camera in the corner. He'd announce his presence when he was good and ready.

Gerald ushered her through a metal door fit with a frosted glass insert. Antiseptic smells and gleaming machines greeted her. An EKG machine, oxygen tanks, defibrillator, pulse oximeter and more. Ten hospital-grade beds occupied the sterile, brightly lit room, and all were empty except for one. A teenage boy was lying asleep in the last bed, his arm in a cast.

Audrey turned her head and found Gerald regarding her with anticipation.

"You have your own private clinic," she said, his intentions starting to take shape.

Black-market medicine. That's what all this turmoil was about.

"Take a look around. You'll see I've stocked it with a variety of equipment."

He stayed close as she ventured farther into the room. Pristine white cabinets, complete with locks, lined the far wall. She wasn't as interested in the supplies as she was the young man. As they neared, she was able to see that his lip was busted and one of his eyes was nearly swollen shut.

"Who's the patient? Someone else who dared cross you?"

He smirked. "I am not in the habit of tending my enemies' injuries." Strolling to stand at the foot of the bed, he said, "This is one of my employees. Ethan's forearm was broken in three places and required surgery."

She assessed his vitals on the screen by the bed. "Did you notice his pulse is elevated?"

"Is that bad?"

"It can indicate he's in pain or dehydrated." The ward had the equipment and supplies necessary for treating life-threatening injuries. What it didn't have was medical personnel. "He needs fluids and someone to monitor his pain levels."

"This is exactly why you're needed, Nurse Harris."

"Can you point me to the intravenous equipment?"

"Unfortunately, I'm not acquainted with the arrangement of supplies."

Hiding her exasperation, she went searching and located pain reliever and Ringer's lactate solution. Within ten minutes, she'd inserted the IV port and administered the medication.

"He looks like he's in high school," she said. "What could he possibly do for you?"

"Ethan is twenty. Young, strong and teachable."

Audrey's stomach churned. During their exploration of the warehouse, she'd glimpsed a staging area with crates containing assault rifles. Her captor had rushed her into another section. Gerald's organization could be involved in more than illegal weapons. Most likely, they dealt in narcotics and other gang-related activities that led to violence and cruelty and untold deaths.

"He has a Navy tattoo. Did he desert?"

He shook his head. "He's a military brat. Believe it or not, military installations are good sources of recruits. Teens are dragged from town to town and many become angry and alienated."

"So you prey on their vulnerability and lure them into a life of crime."

Ethan mumbled and turned his head from side to side.

"Let's give him some privacy." Gerald guided her through a second door and to a window with a one-way view of the ward.

"Don't be quick to judge, Miss Harris. My organization provides a substantial income, not to mention job security, for young men like him. More importantly, we offer what they haven't been able to find in military life—stability and a sense of belonging."

"Do you offer free legal counsel for those who get caught by law enforcement? What about funeral benefits? Tell me, Gerald, how many actually reach retirement age?"

An impatient sigh escaped him. "I expected resistance. I would've liked to give you several days to consider my proposal. However, my son has announced an unexpected visit, and I plan to spend my limited time with him, enjoying his company, not babysitting a beautiful distraction."

A chill raced down her spine, and she regretted speaking her mind. "What proposal?"

"I brought you here to show you the possibility of a different life. A more comfortable life, one beyond your imagination. You see, I'm in need of a nurse who will agree to be available at my convenience. It goes without saying that the compensation would be generous." He studied her from beneath hooded lids. "You have the skills and knowledge I'm looking for, Miss Harris, not to mention dedication. If you were to work for me, you wouldn't have to continue your employment with Onslow General. I have people in place there already, so you would be a free agent. You could say goodbye to that inadequate apartment and find a more suitable place to call home. I own properties across the city. You'd have your pick of them. As for automobiles, well, I can outfit you with one far superior to what you have now."

Audrey gripped the wooden sill around the glass and contemplated the young patient. This had to be a terrible dream.

"You're asking me to use my hard-earned degree and experience to treat criminals," she whispered. Men who'd gotten injured in conflicts with rival gangs or while fleeing police.

"I'm asking you to treat human beings."

"Who willfully hurt others." Perspiration dampened her neck. Her pulse raced. Agreeing to his mad plan went against everything she'd been taught. She couldn't aid his life of crime. "You said you have people at the hospital."

Who could've violated their principles in return for material wealth?

"You will get to work with them, if you say yes."

He scrutinized her with his unnerving, probing gaze. Could Audrey fool a man such as him when every fiber of her being resisted his distasteful proposal?

With an exaggerated grimace, he beckoned the crewcut, thick-necked twins standing guard at the other end of the hallway. They approached, hands flexing and unflexing, as if anticipating wrapping around her throat.

Fear threatened to knock her to the floor. "I didn't give you my answer."

"You didn't have to. You have an expressive face." Tracing her cheek with his fingertip, he said, "You would've been a valuable asset. Such a shame we couldn't come to an agreement."

Flinching away, she gasped when the men seized her arms. "What are you going to do?"

"I'm going to enjoy a late dinner at one of my favorite restaurants. As for you... Sergei and Sasha are going to introduce you to my fer-de-lance." He snickered. "Nasty temperament, that one. Unpredictable."

"S-snake?"

"A pit viper, to be precise. The habitat I've had constructed for him is large and intricate. It resembles his natural environment in South America. He uses heat signatures to locate prey. Your body heat will light up like a beacon. His venom is hemotoxic, which means a slow death as your tissue becomes liquefied and infection sets in."

His evil intent left her speechless. Before she could manage a sane response, the men started forward, forcing her to walk between them. Audrey's struggles were futile. They took her back to the central area that housed the animal exhibits.

When one released her to punch in a door code, she kicked the other one in the groin and yanked free. She didn't make it very far. Sergei—or was it Sasha?—snatched a fistful of her hair and jerked her against his chest. Next thing she knew, she was being lifted in the air.

She was dumped onto a hot, concrete floor in a pitch-black room. The door scraped closed with a bang.

"No!"

Short of breath, her heart nearly bursting from her chest, Audrey scrambled to her feet and pounded on the door.

She abruptly ceased and spun to face the room. What had Gerald said? She'd be a beacon, drawing the venomous snake to her? In the wild, snakes shied away from human contact. This was a captivity situation. She was invading his territory.

The constant ping of trickling water would mask any

sounds he might make. She wouldn't hear his approach. Wouldn't see it.

There was no one around to rescue her. She'd have to figure a way out of this herself.

The video feeds weren't what he'd expected. Leaning over the control-room guy slumped in his chair, Julian looked again. Was this some sort of reptile preserve? He couldn't think of a correlation between Audrey's abduction and illegal animal imports.

A sense of urgency gripped him. This warehouse was a hive of activity. One mistake, and the chances of getting out alive would shrink from slim to none.

His gaze was drawn to the six screens surveilling darkened rooms. Cameras with ultrared technology showed the interior contents using a gray scale. They resembled scenes straight out of the jungle. Artificial waterfalls. Tropical plants and decaying logs. Rocks and soil. Could this be a scientific laboratory of some type?

Julian was about to abandon the control room altogether when he spotted her. There, on the bottom right screen…she stood immobile near the door, pressed flat against the wall, terror stamped on her features.

Julian didn't need to know specifics to know she was in danger. Judging from the building's unusual occupants, he guessed it wasn't a human with a weapon inspiring her fear. What he didn't like was going into a situation blind. Not knowing the exact nature of the threat put him at a disadvantage.

He searched the room for a master panel that controlled the door mechanisms. Nothing. A network of rooms and hallways stood between the control room and the main section. He'd have to think of a distraction.

There. Grabbing the unconscious goon's open soda can, he dumped out the liquid and cut a hole halfway down. He used papers from the cabinets to stuff into the open top. When the can was packed tight, he removed the lighter from the pack of Camel Lights lying near the man's hand and used the flame to light the paper through the lower hole. Smoke curled upward.

He climbed onto an extra chair and held it to the smoke alarm. "Come on, come on."

Finally, the fire alarm pulsed through the building. The resulting chaos would hopefully scramble the men, giving him an opening to extract Audrey. He snagged the fire extinguisher and exited the room. If he couldn't shoot his way in, he'd use the extinguisher to bust through the glass.

He had to reach her before it was too late.

The lights blinked on, temporarily blinding her. She couldn't hear a thing above the shrieking alarm and the blood thundering through her veins. What did it signify? A warning of approaching law enforcement? Or an actual fire somewhere in the facility?

When her eyes adjusted, she scanned the room for signs of the deadly predator. Her knowledge of venomous snakes was limited to East Coast inhabitants. Would the fer-de-lance's scales match the profuse jungle plants or blend in with the soil floor littered with decaying logs?

She had no desire to find out.

Audrey tested the door again, hoping the alarm might've triggered an unlock mechanism. That wasn't the case, so she inched over to inspect the window. There was one weak spot. A chip in the glass. But without a tool or heavy object, she didn't have the means to breach it.

Defeated, she turned back to the room. Despair and fear were a dangerous cocktail. Her thoughts bounced between her dad and Julian. She imagined how distraught Trent would be at her funeral—if he wasn't in jail for tearing Julian limb from limb.

Not happening. Not if I can help it.

"Think, Audrey."

She studied her surroundings again. Then, it came to her. In aquariums and zoos, there was an employee-access point. Gerald said he employed a caretaker. That person would require a place to prepare food and treat sick animals. In order to search for it, she'd have to enter the viper's territory.

It was either that or wait for him to seek her out.

Give me strength, Lord. A verse known the world over came to mind. *Yea, though I walk through the valley of the shadow of death, I will fear no evil; for Thou art with me.*

Forcing her feet into motion, Audrey started for the right wall. The continuing alarm made her ears throb and hindered her ability to concentrate. Her first step over the short rock divider and through shoulder-high plants was a tentative one. A huge leaf snapped back, and she jumped clear off the ground.

Did the snake prefer to lounge on low-hanging branches? Or was he curled into a rock crevice in the manmade waterfall, watching her every move and waiting to strike?

The anticipation of a fatal bite from razor-sharp fangs had sweat pouring off her. There'd be no antivenom. No medical treatment. No pain relief.

Something tickled her neck. She whirled, expecting to be staring into the viper's eyes.

There were eyes, all right, just not the snake's. Beneath the frond, a lean tree frog clung to the hefty stalk.

She sucked humid air into her lungs. Her chest felt tight and heavy.

Resuming her advance, she inspected every inch of the ground around her. The concrete-block walls were painted a murky green. Her feet sank into the thick soil that was interspersed with rocks and broken off leaves and twigs. She neared the waterfall built into the corner. About nine feet tall, water rippled over mossy rocks and gathered in a pool at its base. There was no door and no sign of the snake.

Maneuvering around the waterfall's outer edge, she yelped when her shoe dislodged something solid. She bent down to get a better look and wished she hadn't. It was a man's gold watch that probably belonged to the previous victim.

Her heart wedged into her throat, she rushed toward the long back wall, not as careful in her advancement this time. She wanted out. Now.

Where was that door? Surely there *was* a door!

Audrey shoved aside vegetation rooted in giant terra cotta containers and saw the raised wooden frame, painted green to match the wall, and knob. Three or four strides, and she'd reach it. A fly buzzed around her head. In the middle of shooing it away, she froze. The slow glide in an *S* pattern announced the fer-de-lance's presence.

The triangular-shaped head and distinct pits on either side made her blood run cold.

He was slim and long. Four or five feet. Brown and cream scales. His tail vibrated, and she was sure if the alarm wasn't obliterating every other sound, she would've heard the warning.

When he stopped, he was between her and the door.

Audrey's options were limited and bleak. Waiting around to die wasn't one of them. Taking a couple of deliberate steps in retreat, she snapped a branch off the nearest plant and held it out in front of her. Then she did a slow sidestep toward the door.

Please let this work.

The viper tasted the air with his forked tongue.

She kept moving. When the door was three feet away, she uttered one last prayer and, tossing the branch in the viper's direction, lunged for the knob.

TEN

Audrey vaulted through the opening, not caring where she landed, as long as it was far from the fer-de-lance. She tripped over a cardboard box and slammed into a refrigerator. Scrambling past deep sinks and stainless-steel workstations, she had almost reached the exit when the door creaked open and Julian entered.

Her body went limp with relief. He hadn't given up on her, after all. The instinct to launch herself into his arms was cut off the instant she noticed he wasn't alone. The long-haired guy had a pistol aimed at Julian's head. The twins paraded in behind them, hands flexing again. Finally, Gerald entered, a smug smile on his face.

"I commend you for your quick thinking, Miss Harris. A bit naive of you to assume you'd manage to escape the complex, but courageous all the same."

Audrey locked gazes with Julian. His face was a controlled mask, the look in his eyes unreadable. It scared her that he could bury every emotion. Did he have a plan? Or was he resigned to their fate?

The alarm fell silent.

"Aren't you worried what the fire department will find when they respond to that?" she said.

"I have people across the city on my payroll." Gerald had a wallet in his hand. He opened it and commenced pulling out the cards, tossing each one on the floor until he got to the last. He flashed a green ID card. "Your bodyguard is a marine. Should've known. They're a dime a dozen around here."

He dropped the ID onto the tiles with the other cards

and turned to the long-haired man. "Josef, prepare the boat. I want the three of you to take our guests on a deep-sea excursion." To Julian and Audrey, he said, "Not all of my cultivated relationships with law enforcement are rock-solid. On the off chance they do pay us a visit, it's best you aren't seen on the premises."

Josef swiftly went to do his boss's bidding. "Sasha, you're in charge of this one." The one with a diamond in his right ear seized Julian and propelled him into the hall.

"Wait." Audrey rushed after them. Sergei's beefy hand encircled her upper arm. He stuck a gun against her ribs.

"No funny business this time," he growled, urging her through the doorway.

"Give my regards to the sharks," Gerald called, maniacal laughter echoing after them.

They were led to the staging area, where huge garage doors had been opened and moving vans backed up to loading docks. The men packing and loading crates gave them scant attention. Josef removed a set of keys from a metal panel and hopped onto the pavement beside one of the vans. The twins corralled Julian and her into a rear corner and stationed themselves a few feet away.

He spoke without looking at her. "You hurt?"

"No." Beyond the vans, she could see Josef trotting toward a dock. "How did you find me?"

"You took too long in the restroom. I searched and found your scarf." He clamped his mouth shut when Sasha shifted his ice-blue gaze in their direction. When the hulking man looked away, Julian said, "I was in time to see the catering van peel out. Tailed them to this business district."

She fit her hand into his warm, calloused one. "Thank you."

A muscle jerked in his jaw. "It was a mistake not to involve law enforcement."

"There wasn't time." She squeezed his hand. "You're here with me now."

"We're going to have to wait until we get on the water to make our move."

Audrey did not like the sound of that. While she'd grown up in beach towns, she preferred the coastline and the reassurance of solid ground beneath her feet. Being miles from shore? Not her idea of fun.

"Julian—"

Sergei interrupted their conversation. Grabbing her again, he pushed her toward the door. "Time for a boat ride."

She glanced over her shoulder. Sasha had his gun on Julian.

"Your friend's coming, too," he said in his thick accent.

"You and your brother worked for Gerald long?"

Maybe their loyalty to the crime boss could be weakened.

He didn't answer.

"Have you had to murder other innocent people for him?"

His lips pinched. He led her to a metal door beside the open bays and down a set of concrete steps. They walked toward the river, where Josef was already readying the yacht. Moths danced in the circle of a lamp. The cover of darkness would make their nefarious task infinitely easier.

Knots formed in her midsection. "Gerald would never know if you let us go. You could drop us off at a random dock somewhere."

In response, he produced zip ties, which he used to bind her wrists. Behind them, Sasha did the same to Julian.

"At least tell me who's been helping him with the wounded."

He stepped back. "Accept your fate. No use fighting the inevitable."

"But—"

"Hush."

When they forced them to board, the vessel's slight rocking unnerved her. Josef emerged from the bridge and tapped his earpiece.

"There's a problem with one of the van drivers. Boss needs me here."

The brothers exchanged a look. "See you in a couple of hours."

Sasha pointed to the stairs that led below deck. "Keep an eye on them while I oversee navigation."

Sergei held his hands up, palms out. "You want me stuck in the head losing my dinner? That is what will happen if I'm trapped down there."

"I forgot." He muttered something in another language. "You should've learned how to captain a boat."

"I'll add ties around their ankles. They won't be a threat."

"Fine. Hurry up."

Sergei motioned with his gun. Julian descended the stairs first. Audrey's nerves stretched thin as she followed him down into the dim galley area. It was smaller than her apartment kitchen. The ceiling hovered too close to her head. Her breathing became shallow.

Julian turned and shot her a look, but she couldn't decipher it in the faint light. A single bulb above the stove did little to dispel the shadows.

Both brothers entered the galley. Sasha hung back, his gun trained on them, while Sergei ordered them on the floor and placed zip ties around their ankles. They returned to the deck and slammed the door at the top of the stairs shut. Seconds later, the engine's rumble shook the floor beneath her.

Her throat began to close up.

Julian rolled onto his side, facing her. "Breathe, Audrey."

"Is this a bad time to tell you I'm a terrible swimmer?"

He was silent a beat. "On the off chance we wind up in the water, just remember to pedal like you're on a bicycle. When you get tired, float on your back."

"With restraints on?"

Maneuvering onto his knees, he used his mouth to pull the ties around his wrists tighter, and then he brought his arms up and down in one fluid motion, snapping the locking mechanism.

"How did you do that?"

"I'll explain later."

He flicked on an overhead light and rummaged through the drawers until he located a knife. The yacht's speed increased, which meant they were leaving civilization behind.

"How long do you think we have?" she asked, watching as he sawed through the tie around his ankles.

"Could be a half hour or more. Depends on how much boat traffic is out tonight. Hold out your wrists." He made short work of freeing her. When he helped her to stand, she fought the impulse to cling to him, to find solace in his arms. There was no softness in him at the moment. The overhead light cast his features in sharp, statue-like relief. He was in survival mode, as she should be.

"What's your plan?"

Peering out of the lone, skinny window, he eyed the horizon. "You stay put while I deal with the twins."

The vessel hit rough water, and the floor dipped and swayed. Audrey clutched the marble counter for balance. His path toward the stairs brought him to where she stood.

Putting a hand on his chest, she peered into his face. "Isn't there anything I can do to help? Create a distraction?"

Sighing, he gingerly smoothed her hair behind her ear and trailed his fingers to rest against the side of her nape. "You can help by staying out of sight so I won't worry about you."

The unexpected caress scattered chill bumps across her shoulders. She realized her error in judgment. Julian wasn't an emotionless robot. He'd simply mastered the ability to bury his feelings. Did he care about her? Or was this merely a bid for redemption? A chance to assuage misplaced guilt?

"You expect me to do all the worrying, huh?"

"I'll be back in five minutes." Placing the knife into her hand, he said, "Lock yourself in the cabin and wait for me."

She tried to give it back. "You'll need this."

Shaking his head, he strode for the stairs. He stopped halfway up. "Audrey, go."

"Yes, Sergeant."

Checking her watch, she did as he instructed. But imagining what might be happening above deck was torture. Julian had suffered physical and emotional trauma and was deep in the grief process. She wouldn't be able to forgive herself if he got injured while she was cowering in the sleeping quarters.

With a death grip on the knife, she left the minuscule space and climbed the stairs. Audrey eased the door open. The seating area was empty, of course. She hadn't expected the brothers to be lounging around eating chocolate-covered strawberries. Her stomach rumbled. She'd missed Lincoln and Chasity's elegant dinner. The couple must be confused and upset over her and Julian's disappearance.

She offered up a silent request for protection. Moonlight glinted off the water. The glittering shoreline was growing smaller. A fine mist coated her skin as she rounded the corner and navigated the narrow walkway leading to the bridge. The sound of the bow slicing through waves prevented her from hearing what was happening up ahead. She crept closer to the opening in the bulkhead on her right.

When she finally reached the bridge, the sight of Julian facing off against the hulking twins made her gasp.

Blood trickled from a slash on his cheek as he ducked Sergei's fist and twisted out of Sasha's reach. Spinning around with the grace of a seasoned martial artist, he landed a kick to Sergei's ribs. The man doubled over. His brother lunged again for Julian and managed to seize his injured arm. Seeing Julian's wince, the giant locked on with both hands and squeezed.

Audrey didn't think about consequences. She charged into the fray, managing to get an arm locked around Sasha's neck. She tugged with all her might.

"Audrey, no!"

Sasha flung her off with little effort. She glanced off a fixed chair on her way to the floor. Sergei advanced. She scrambled backward.

Too little, too late. He yanked her up and tossed her over his shoulder. A few strides later, she felt herself flying backward. She opened her mouth to scream. Icy black water swallowed her whole. The shock caused her to freeze. She began to sink.

Bicycle. Think bicycle.

Locking onto the memory of Julian's advice and his utter calm under fire, she tamped down the rising panic and moved her arms and legs in a methodical pattern. Her head broke through the surface, and she gulped in cold air.

Scraping the hair out of her eyes, she saw the boat skimming through the waves, leaving her alone in the vast sea.

Julian prided himself on his ability to maintain control, no matter the situation. It's what he'd been trained to do. Forget emotion and focus on the task at hand. Fear, disgust, worry—they weakened him. He'd heeded his instructors and mentors and learned to sift through his experiences after the fact. Postsituational purging, they had called it.

Audrey was the wild card. The unknown variable that obliterated objective, logical thought.

The instant Sergei had put his hands on her, a switch flipped inside him. Rage channeling through his veins, Julian struck Sasha's windpipe at the precise angle to induce unconsciousness. He didn't wait to see him hit the deck. Spinning, he met Sergei's advance head-on, grabbing the man's collar and pulling him close before he slammed his upper body into the glass windshield. Another perfectly aimed jab rendered him useless.

Julian jumped to the controls, located the throttle and slowed the engine. Guiding the vessel in a sharp U-turn, he began the painstaking search.

Audrey needs You, God. Protect her. Please.
Lead me to her.

This self-appointed mission was no longer about duty or gratitude. He genuinely liked Audrey Harris. Somehow, she'd breached the cloud of self-pity and sorrow he'd used to insulate himself. She'd made him care again.

His gaze swept the inky sea before him. Despite the warm days they'd enjoyed this month, the water would be cold enough to induce hypothermia. And by her own account, she wasn't the best swimmer. If she gave in to panic...

Fingers tightening on the wheel, he leaned closer to the

windshield, as if the extra inches would make it possible for him to locate her. Minutes passed. There was no sign of her. Despair flung him back to the accident site. He'd dragged his teammates out of the helo, away from the smoke and fire. He'd performed CPR. Fashioned tourniquets. He'd done everything humanly possible to save them.

"Don't let her die, God." The plea ripped from his lips.

Audrey was young and vibrant, a shining light of compassion in a hurting world. She was beautiful and brave.

Killing the engine, he dashed outside and called her name. He went to the stern and did the same. Then to the starboard side.

Above the slapping of water against the boat's hull, he heard it. Her voice. Faint but strong.

"Audrey!"

Far from the craft, beyond the circle of light generated by the spotlight, he spotted something pale and gleaming. Her sweater.

Diving in, he propelled himself through the water to where she floated on her back.

"Julian." Her colorless lips trembled in a failed attempt at a smile. Letting her legs lower in the water, she moved into an upright position. "Thank God you found me."

"I wouldn't have abandoned you." His voice sounded strange to his own ears. He curled his arm around her, taking her weight and giving her a chance to rest. "Relax, okay. Let me guide you."

Sighing, she nodded, her trusting gaze gulping in the sight of him. He had to resist the urge to caress her cheek and crush her to him. Now wasn't the time to celebrate. They weren't out of danger yet.

Julian helped her onto the boat. Audrey snuck her arms around his waist and burrowed against his chest. He didn't immediately react. Then, silencing the warnings in his head, he held her. They were both dripping wet and shivering, but this wasn't about seeking physical warmth. This was solace. Gratitude. Relief. This was friendship. Trust. A bond forged through trials.

As he gently rubbed her back and found his way to her silken nape, she lifted her cheek from his chest and gazed up at him with unconcealed longing. An answering call was born inside.

This could *not* become more than friendship. Anything romantic with Audrey would not be casual. He sensed it in his bones.

So he swallowed the disappointment threatening to choke him and, placing his hands on her shoulders, gently set her away.

"I have to deal with the twins."

She bit her lip. Her hair was plastered to her head and her elegant clothes had a ragged appearance. Her lashes swept down, concealing her thoughts from him. She folded her arms over her middle and nodded. "What then?"

"We get to shore and connect with the authorities."

"And then it's over?"

"I wish I could tell you what you want to hear."

They were being pursued by a crime boss with widespread connections. Gerald had hospital employees on his payroll. Fire-department personnel, too. He wasn't about to let them go free, not when they could pinpoint his base of operations and bear witness to his illegal activities.

"I'm not after platitudes," she stated. "I want the truth."

"It's not over. Not by a long shot."

ELEVEN

She was miserable.

Audrey huddled beneath the rough blanket Julian had scrounged from a storage compartment and tried to avoid staring at his profile. Seated on the thin carpet, her back wedged into the corner, she couldn't see the ocean or the night sky from her vantage point. What else of interest was there besides her rescuer?

He stood proud and stoic at the helm, seemingly oblivious to her presence. He'd retreated physically and emotionally—which meant he'd read something in her eyes that had either scared or disgusted him.

Audrey scooped the wet hair off her shoulders and twisted it into a rope. Her damp clothes clung to her skin, and her stomach, though queasy, wasn't happy about not being fed for half the day. A long shower, change of clothes and hot meal were probably hours away. Julian had used the radio to contact the authorities. They'd instructed them where to dock and had promised to have a patrol car waiting. The identical goons were bound with duct tape and locked below deck.

Julian looked as handsome as ever, despite the fresh bruises, the scrape on his cheek and a tear in the shoulder of his dress shirt. He'd shucked his suit coat somewhere, probably for more ease of movement.

Why had she collapsed in his arms? Why couldn't she have simply offered him a handshake or hearty pat on the back as a way to express her thanks?

Audrey tried to tell herself it had been a natural reaction to stress, that she would've reached out to whoever was nearby and sympathetic. She couldn't quite believe it. Despite her reservations about romance and her reluctance to open herself up again, she'd developed an attachment to Julian Tan. Admiration had transformed into something more meaningful.

Thankfully, she wasn't in too deep. She wasn't ready. When she *did* make the conscious choice to love someone again, it wouldn't be a man who courted danger on and off the job. A combat-ready marine as her significant other? Not going to happen. Watching Seth suffer and ultimately succumb to illness had deadened part of her heart. While no one was immune to disease, she intended to play it as safe as possible. Audrey pictured herself with a steadfast, nice but unadventurous guy with a nonhazardous career. Her dad approved of the plan.

"We're almost there." Julian's voice snapped her out of her ruminations. "The police will want to hear our accounts of what's happened. It probably won't be a brief process."

She let her hair fall into place, stood and folded the blanket. The salty breeze whistling through the bridge raised goose bumps across her skin. Joining him at the controls, she rested against a chair. They were close enough to shore that she could see inside the few waterfront homes with lights still on. It was approaching 2:00 a.m.

"I won't mind being surrounded by law enforcement," she said. "At least we'll be safe."

Julian didn't reply. His sideways glance quickly took her measure. Before she could ask what was on his mind, he pointed to the restaurant dock ahead.

"They're waiting on us."

A pair of patrol cars, parked nose-to-nose, were visible in the otherwise deserted parking lot.

"I don't see the Coast Guard."

He shrugged. "Must've beat them here."

When he'd carefully maneuvered the vessel into a slip and secured it with thick ropes, he took her hand and assisted her onto the dock.

"You need to go to the hospital and get your arm examined," she told him.

"It's fine."

The officers—one redheaded and freckled and the other shorter than Audrey—strode down the slanted walkway to meet them.

"Julian Tan?" The redheaded officer spoke first.

"Yes, sir."

His watery blue eyes pinned Audrey. "And you are?"

"Audrey Harris. I don't have identification. My things are at the house where I was abducted. The owner, Dr. Lincoln Fitzgerald, will confirm our identities."

"Mine was confiscated, as well," Julian said. "The men who forced us onto the boat are locked in the cabin."

The short, balding officer boarded the boat. "They aren't armed, I'm assuming, since you were able to restrain them."

"No, sir. I placed their weapons in the bridge." He detailed where the officer could locate them.

The officer opened the cabin door and, gun in his grip, descended the stairs.

"Do either of you need immediate medical assistance?"

They turned back to the redhead, whose tone conveyed concern.

"Sergeant Tan recently had surgery," Audrey said. "He needs to be seen."

She prayed he wouldn't get an infection or require a third surgery.

"It can wait until we've given our statements."

He nodded. "Good. Why don't you wait by the cruisers while I have a word with Officer Dunn?"

They proceeded up the walkway and onto the restaurant's generous deck. Her stomach rumbled. "I wish they were open for business," she said, passing darkened plate-glass windows.

"I haven't eaten here before, but my buddy brings his wife here every weekend." His head dipped. "I mean he used to. Before…"

Audrey longed to take his hand. But after his reaction to her show of affection, she resisted.

"You'll have to give it a try sometime," she said lightly, hoping he didn't think she was insinuating anything.

At the patrol cars, they waited in tense silence for the officer to return. After what seemed to her like a very long time, he rounded the corner alone.

"Dunn is going to remain here until transport arrives. I'll take you down to the station." Opening the rear door, he said, "I'm Officer Craddock, by the way."

Audrey slid in first. Julian settled in next, leaving plenty of space between them. She stared out her window, determined not to be bothered. If she got the chance, she'd inform him that he wasn't her type and that he had nothing to be worried about.

When they were speeding along the street, Craddock said, "You'll be happy I cleaned out my cruiser yesterday. It can get nasty really quick."

"I've never ridden in a police car," she said to fill the silence.

Beside her, Julian was lost in thought. Or was he taking in details? Hard to tell.

The heater's comforting warmth, combined with the smooth ride down the rural road, made Audrey drowsy. Unable to hold her head up any longer, she closed her eyes and rested against the seat. She wasn't sure how much time had passed when Julian's hand closed over hers and squeezed three times. The gesture startled her at first. It was a throwback to her childhood—her mom and dad's way to say "I love you" without speaking a word.

Of course, he wasn't trying to communicate such a thing. She lifted her head to look over at him. His quick, furtive look gave her little to go on.

"What's wrong?"

Releasing her, he shifted forward in the seat, massaged his forehead and groaned. "I'm going be sick."

Instantly concerned, she placed her hand lightly on his back. "Are you experiencing any other symptoms besides nausea?"

"My head's killing me. I need fresh air."

Audrey gripped the seat in front of them. "Is there anywhere we can pull over for a few minutes?"

Craddock's washed-out eyes met hers in the rearview mirror. "We'll be at the station shortly. There are vending machines. I'm sure a cold soda would help calm his stomach."

She didn't recognize the passing scenery of night-draped woods and the occasional house, but she hadn't been paying attention.

Julian groaned again. "You're going to have to reclean your car if you don't pull over soon."

When the officer didn't respond, Audrey spoke up. "I'm a registered nurse, and I recognize the signs of distress. Please, there's hardly any traffic on this road. Can't we find a spot to get out for a minute?"

With a frustrated grunt, he slowed the vehicle and pulled onto the shoulder. "You've got five minutes."

The officer got out. The headlight beams became distorted as he walked past the hood.

"What's his problem?" she wondered aloud.

"Audrey—"

Craddock opened Julian's door and switched on his powerful flashlight. "Watch your step."

Julian climbed out and shuffled a short distance away. Audrey exited after him. Worry distracted her as she ran through a mental list of ailments.

She started to join him.

"Don't come close," he ordered gruffly. Turning away, he crouched over a shallow ditch.

She remained behind the open door. "I'd like to help."

He dismissed her with a wave. "Can you not shine that thing on me, Officer? A little privacy would be nice."

After a long moment, Craddock complied, pointing the light onto his feet. "Nothing to be embarrassed about. I see this type of thing a lot."

"Do you see this?"

Julian sprung up from his crouched position and used the forward motion of his body to knock Craddock into the side of the car. Audrey screamed and jumped out of the way.

"Julian?"

"Run, Audrey!"

The officer retaliated and dragged Julian to the ground. The pair rolled into the cone of light supplied by the dropped flashlight. Craddock landed a hard blow to Julian's face. Unfazed, he used his legs to maneuver himself into the superior position. He went for Craddock's weapon. Again, the officer's balled fist connected with Julian. His temple area, this time.

Audrey slapped her hand over her mouth as Julian hung his head and blinked several times, then slowly crawled out of reach. She had no clue why he'd attacked the officer, but she trusted him one-hundred-percent.

When Craddock pulled his gun and aimed it at Julian's back, everything inside her rose up in protest. She sprinted toward him. He swiveled. Time slowed. In the darkness, his eyes gleamed like a madman's. He *relished* the chance to kill her.

She skidded in the sandy, roadside soil.

Julian's rage-filled growl penetrated the roaring in her ears. He rammed into Craddock. A shot ripped through the night. The bullet whizzed past her shoulder.

In a matter of seconds, Craddock was facedown on the ground.

Shock held Audrey in place. Julian jammed his knee between Craddock's shoulder blades and used the man's own handcuffs on him.

"You're a dead man," the officer snarled, trying to twist free.

Julian calmly emptied Craddock's service weapon and tossed the bullets into the grass. "I'm not the only one with a target on my back. You had a job to do, and you failed. Tell me, Craddock, what does Gerald do with men who can't follow orders?"

His body went slack. "I don't know what you're talking about."

"Don't you?" Fishing through his pockets, Julian produced a cell phone. "What am I going to find? Texts? Emails? Is Officer Dunn on Gerald's payroll, too?"

His lips thinned, and he said nothing.

Audrey's knees grew weak. "How did you know?"

After powering down the cell phone and removing s the battery, he tucked it into his pocket. "We have to move. I'll explain on the way."

"You can't hide," Craddock said almost gleefully. "Not with modern technology."

"Same goes for you," Julian quipped. "Get up."

Once the officer was on his feet, Julian thrust him into the backseat.

"You'll have law enforcement descending on this area the moment I'm discovered. You'll be fugitives—"

Julian shut the door. He popped the car hood and started ripping out wires. Audrey looked up and down the road, unwilling to imagine what would happen if someone came upon this scene. Not that it mattered. Their fingerprints were everywhere. Craddock would spin whatever tale suited his purposes.

"He's right, you know. On top of Gerald's army, we're going to have every single law-enforcement officer in this area searching for us."

"That's why we have to get moving." Lowering the hood, he threaded his fingers through hers and urged her into motion. "I'll get Craddock's phone to a buddy of mine. Let's hope he's either too careless or too arrogant to have erased evidence of his connection to Gerald."

"If there isn't any..." The prospect of jail time loomed.

His grip tightened. "We'll find another way to link them."

He led her away from the road and into a farm field.

"I didn't detect anything suspicious about him," she said, feeling foolish. "What tipped you off?"

Dried cornstalks crunched beneath their feet. " Craddock didn't take the turnoff to the station. While you were resting, I pretended to snooze. He flew past the downtown area and headed toward Richlands."

Audrey replayed the recent scene. She'd seen Craddock's expression. He'd been poised to shoot Julian in the back. Sure, Julian had started the altercation, but he'd been dazed and struggling in that moment. And she couldn't forget he'd actually shot at her, and barely missed.

"I waited for him to make a stop," he said. "Maybe

at a gas station or even a fast-food place, before turning around and heading to the station. The more miles he put between us and the city, the more convinced I became that he had other plans in mind. When he lied to you, my suspicions were confirmed."

"So you pretended to be sick."

"Yes."

Audrey thanked God that Julian had heeded his instincts. If he hadn't, Craddock would've disposed of them, leaving Gerald to continue preying on military kids and putting hospital patients at risk.

TWELVE

Furious barking erupted somewhere to their left, and Audrey nearly jumped out of her skin. A light blinked on, flooding the house's rear yard.

"Looks like we disturbed the farmer's guard dog," Julian said, increasing the pace.

The woods they were heading for weren't far off. Would they reach them before the owner greeted them with a shotgun?

"I don't have any treats to use as a bribe," she said, picturing sharp canines and claws. "Where are we going, anyway? Once day breaks, there will be few places to hide. Are you familiar with Richlands?"

The farming community was farther inland than Jacksonville, and she hadn't had cause to frequent it other than a yearly visit to the pumpkin patch.

They entered the woods, and the barking ceased. Audrey glanced over her shoulder. There were no irate home owners bearing down on them. Yet.

"I've visited friends who live in the area, and I've driven this direction when I've had flights to catch in and out of Jacksonville. Do I know exactly what's on the other side of these woods? No."

They dodged tree trunks and decaying logs. She wished she'd worn tennis shoes and workout gear to Lincoln and Chasity's party. Adding to her body's various aches and pains, her toes and heels throbbed in the ballet-style flats.

"We'll find a place to hunker down for a few hours, then we'll search for a way to contact my buddy, Brady.

I wish we could use Craddock's phone, but I don't want to risk anyone tracing our location. When I do manage to speak to him, I'll arrange for him to bring us cash and clothing."

"And food."

"Definitely." A light laugh escaped, an unexpected and pleasant sound.

"I didn't get a chance to ask what was in that room with you."

A shudder worked its way down her spine. "Pit viper. Gerald called it a fer-de-lance."

He squeezed her hand once. "You're a brave woman."

"I don't feel like I am."

"I've seen you in action. Believe me, you've handled everything that's been thrown at you with pure grit."

Tears smarted. "Before this, the most challenging thing in my life was watching my fiancé battle cancer and not being able to do a single thing to help him."

"The young man in the photograph?"

"Seth."

"He didn't make it?"

"He fought long and hard for five years. Had several remissions, but it was persistent."

"I'm sorry. Watching people suffer and being powerless to save them is devastating."

"You did everything you could, Julian."

"Did I?" His voice brimmed with self-reproach.

"What the media reports left out, my dad filled in. You risked your life pulling those men out of the burning wreckage and administering first aid until the EMTs arrived. What more could you have done?"

"Lots of things. Moved faster. Pulled them out in different order. Treated their injuries in a more efficient way."

"You were injured, don't forget, and probably suffering from shock."

An owl hooted above their heads. Beneath their feet, twigs snapped and dead leaves crunched. They walked through the copse without speaking.

"I can't wrap my head around the fact that I survived, and they didn't."

This glimpse of his immense sorrow humbled Audrey. "I wish I had answers for you. Some magic words that would wipe away your pain. All I have is my faith in God, Who is loving and just and wise. His Word instructs us to cast our burdens and hurts on Him, and He will comfort us."

"He didn't hear my pleas that day."

Hurting for him, she traced her thumb over his knuckles. "He did, Julian. Just like He heard mine throughout Seth's long ordeal. He simply chose to answer our prayers in a way we didn't want or understand."

She sensed rather than saw him shake his head. Since he didn't voice his thoughts, she had no way of knowing the effect of her words. As they put more distance between themselves and the farmhouse, she asked the Lord to give him peace and comfort. She also prayed for wisdom and protection. Things were bound to get harder before they got better.

Julian contemplated the massive pond they'd stumbled upon in the midst of fallow fields. They'd left the woods behind an hour ago and had yet to reach another road or dwelling. He could hike indefinitely. He was used to dealing with gnawing hunger and fatigue. Audrey was another story. She was tough, he'd give her that. There'd been no complaints. No sighs or grumbling. But she'd grown quiet, and he couldn't overlook her slowed pace or the frequent shivers wracking her frame.

The moon's reflection bobbed on the mirrorlike surface. Its faint light outlined a wooden structure at the pond's edge. "Let's check that out."

"I thought we would keep going until we found a means for you to contact your friend."

"Better to rest for an hour or two while we can."

It was a calculated risk. There was no way to predict how much time would pass before Officer Craddock was discovered. He might or might not sic the authorities on them, depending on how Gerald typically wanted situations like this handled.

"Don't stop for me," she said. "I'll tell you when I can't take another step."

"We can't approach any homes in the middle of the night asking to use a phone. I was hoping to come across a gas station by now. There's bound to be a customer who'll take pity on a pair of stranded sweethearts."

"Sweethearts?"

"We have to have a convincing backstory. Look at us."

Frowning, she flicked a strand of hair out of her eyes. "I suppose."

"Don't worry. No kissing required."

"That's a relief."

An awkward tension settled between them. What he'd meant as a joke had fallen flat, probably because they were both aware of the attraction brewing between them. Had he been tempted to kiss her for real? Absolutely. Would he give in to that impulse? He couldn't be sure. Doing so would be foolhardy. Not only because of her father's express wishes, but also because Audrey was a special person. He wouldn't dream of toying with her emotions.

Yawning, she reached behind her and kneaded her lower back muscles. Decision made.

"One hour," he said, striding for the shelter. "We can afford one hour."

Audrey didn't argue. Flicking on the flashlight, he was glad to see the interior of the boat-storage area was in decent shape. There weren't any cushions or blankets, but at least they'd be tucked out of sight.

They found spots and relaxed against the side wall. A wide shaft of filmy moonlight fell through the opening. Audrey groaned and, slipping off her flimsy shoes, started to massage her feet through the thin socks.

"Let me do that."

"That's not necess—"

Julian brushed aside her hands and took over for her. Her eyes drifted closed, and a contented sigh escaped.

"Now that's a useful skill in a fellow fugitive," she quipped.

"During high school, my sisters begged me to massage their feet after long shifts at their part-time retail jobs. I agreed. For a small fee, of course."

"You are *that* brother, huh?"

Her eyes were still closed, and she used the wall for support. Slowly, the tension seemed to leave her body. Julian assumed she'd dozed off.

Suddenly, she stiffened. "We're near water."

He removed his hands. "What's wrong?"

Lifting her head, she glanced around. "It's dark. Lots of undisturbed nooks and crannies for snakes to hide."

This was her first chance to rest, and her mind must've begun a replay of events. He placed his hand on her knee and squeezed. "They aren't usually active during winter months, but I'll take a look around."

Switching on the flashlight, he got up and looked

around the stacked kayaks and paddles. He inspected all the corners, too. Nothing but cobwebs and dead insects.

"You can relax," he said, returning to her side. "This shelter is officially a reptile-free zone."

He saw her smile. "Beneath that marine-hero armor, you're a really sweet guy."

"My sisters would have something to say about that."

"I would argue the point if they cared to discuss it with me," she vowed, pulling on her flats. In a more subdued voice, she said, "Do you have a plan for what's next? If you're required to medically retire?"

"No." He couldn't bring himself to consider an alternate life other than the one he'd been leading.

"You wouldn't want to return to Hawaii full-time?"

"And live under the shadow of Chin Tan's disapproval? No, thanks. Besides, it's not cheap to live there. I have no idea what career I'd pursue. The Marine Corps is my life, and I assumed it always would be."

He'd been taught to think outside the box, to expect the unexpected during missions. He'd failed to apply that lesson to the civilian side of life, leaving him reeling and unprepared for a future that suddenly wasn't written in stone.

"Maybe it's time to consider other options," she ventured. "If we don't wind up behind bars. Or worse."

"That's not going to happen."

"I wish I had your confidence. Usually, I'm a glass-half-full kind of girl, but lately—"

She stopped talking and cocked her head. The unmistakable sound of dogs barking pierced the stillness. Julian stood to his feet. That was the sound of a hunt. And he and Audrey were the prize.

THIRTEEN

"Run!"

Julian seized Audrey's hand and broke into a sprint.

"Is it the police?" she gasped. "Already?"

"It's possible."

Resting hadn't been the safe choice, after all. He was starting to wonder if he'd lost his touch.

They circled the pond and entered an overgrown field. His night-vision goggles would come in handy right about now.

"They're getting closer!" Audrey gripped his hand more tightly.

He couldn't stand the thought of her suffering any more than she already had. Releasing her hand, he slowed. "Keep going. I'll distract them."

Her eyes widened. "No, Julian."

"Yes." He stopped running. "Remember this number. Brady will help you. Nine-one-zero—"

"I'm not leaving you." Jutting her chin, she glared at him. "We're in this together."

Lights bounced over them, and within seconds, he could see a trio of bloodhounds baying and frothing at the mouth. Julian moved to stand in front of Audrey and held out his arms. They'd have to go through him to get to her, and he wasn't about to make it easy.

A single ATV lurched to a stop several yards away. The driver let loose a shrill whistle that silenced the dogs. He approached with rifle in hand.

"You think you can trespass on my land and get away with it?" Outrage distorted the elderly man's wizened face.

"I'm fed up with you people using my property to do your drugs and drink your booze." He aimed his rifle at them.

"We apologize for trespassing, sir," Julian said. "We're not using your land as a party site."

"Oh, yeah? What were you doing in my boat storage, then?"

"We've attracted the attention of serious criminals who aim to silence us."

He grunted. "Likely story."

"It's the truth." Audrey edged out from behind him. "Don't you recognize him? He's the only survivor of the training accident at Camp Lejeune. Sergeant Julian Tan."

Squinting at Julian, he jerked a nod. "Read about it in the papers."

"I'm a nurse at Onslow General. Julian serves in the same unit as my father. That's how we met. Oh, and we live in the same apartment complex."

"Hmph." He eyed them with misgiving.

"Actually, Audrey was my postsurgical nurse. She saved my life when someone tried to kill me."

Audrey glanced over at Julian. "And then he saved mine. Multiple times. We're in a lot of trouble, sir. Will you help us?"

He lowered the rifle and rubbed a weary hand down his face. "This is too much nonsense for me to make heads or tails of."

"Can we at least use your phone to make a call?" Audrey said.

"If what you say is true, I want no part of it." He flung a gnarled hand toward the east. "Get off my land before I decide to call the cops."

"But—"

Julian closed his hand over her shoulder. "It's okay,"

he murmured. To the irate farmer, he said, "Which way to the nearest road and gas station?"

Again, he pointed east. When they were out of earshot, she said, "He didn't believe us, did he?"

"We roused him out of a warm bed. He's grumpy and confused."

"Maybe."

The disillusion in her voice troubled him. He put his arm around her and pulled her close to his side as they continued to walk.

"Before you know it, you'll be back tending to patients and dominating the volleyball court. All of this will be an unpleasant memory."

To his surprise, she settled her arm around his waist, linking them further. "I hope you're right, Sergeant."

They walked until Audrey thought she couldn't go on. Every time she opened her mouth to tell Julian, she thought about those hounds and how they could've been K-9 dogs trained to take down suspects. She was dirty, thirsty and ravenous. As the sky above lightened to lilac, she contemplated the ground around them, wondering if there were any edible plants that might've sprung up early.

"If you could have any meal right now, what it would be?" she asked.

A smile eased his somber countenance. "Poke."

"Never heard of it."

"It's a raw fish salad."

"Raw fish? I don't know."

"It's delicious."

"I'll take your word for it."

"You should at least try it. The yellowfin tuna is my favorite. I can prepare it for you sometime. Won't be as good as what you'd get in Hawaii, but you'd get to sample it."

"I'd like that."

The sun peeked over the horizon, casting a golden pink hue over the flat landscape. She looked over at Julian and was again awestruck by his physical appeal. The impact he had on her went beyond his looks, however. He'd become important to her personally. Precious. Treasured. The depth of her admiration and affection for him had blossomed in a short amount of time, thanks to their unique circumstances. She couldn't begin to guess how he felt about her. His offer meant he wouldn't banish her from his life, at least.

"Your turn," he said, his gaze roaming her face.

What did he see? Gerald had claimed her thoughts were easy to read. She wished Julian wasn't a pro at masking his.

"I'd have to go with classic lasagna and garlic knots. Garden salad on the side."

He nodded. "Italian is a good choice."

Because he was looking at her, he didn't see the cement-block building ahead.

"Julian."

They'd not only reached a road, but there was also a convenience store. They stopped and considered the sight. The paint was faded and peeling, and the sign damaged. A single car was parked on the cracked blacktop.

His features sharpened. "We have to be convincing. No mention of our actual names or circumstances."

"I remember." They'd discussed it at length. Licking her dry lips, she tried to calm her nerves. "I'm going to duck into the bathroom while you ask to use the phone."

"We act suspicious, people get ideas."

"Right," she said. "We act innocent."

He cupped her upper arms. "We *are* innocent."

She blew out a measured breath. "I know."

"You good?"

"As long as I don't come near the slushy machine, I'm good."

"I promise to buy you a year's supply of cherry slushies once this is over."

"Poke bowls and slushies. You're making big promises, Sergeant."

"I don't make promises I don't keep." He winked and, leaning in, kissed her forehead.

She might've fainted then and there if he hadn't taken her hand and led her through the scrubby grass to the store. They entered through a side entrance door. The cashier counter was vacant.

Warmth washed over her, heating her chilled skin.

"Coffee," she murmured, sniffing the air. "Is that *bacon* I smell?"

"Patience," he whispered in her ear, gently prodding her down the first aisle. The sign for the restrooms beckoned.

A morning news announcement coming from the television affixed above the counter chased thoughts of their plan from her mind. The anchor read off their names as photographs of her and Julian flashed on the screen.

She swayed.

Julian's arm came around her, steadying her. "Nothing has changed." His voice was low and forceful. "Stick to the plan."

She bowed her head and pressed her hand to her middle. The smells that had been tantalizing a minute ago now made her feel ill.

"Audrey." There was a clash of urgency, worry and demand in that one word.

He was depending on her *not* to fall apart.

"I'm good."

Shrugging off his arm, she squared her shoulders, held her head high and strode to the restroom. Once inside, she let the tears flow.

* * *

He didn't like where this was headed. Not one bit. Dirty cops in league with territorial crime lords equaled major trouble. If he and Audrey didn't find a safe, discreet place to lay low, it wouldn't be long before they were recognized.

Julian casually perused the snacks. The rounded mirror in the corner reflected a skewed image of the four aisles and refrigerated coolers along the back wall. Still no sign of the employee. Striding to the television, he reached up and turned it off. He could only pray that report hadn't been playing on a loop the entire night.

A door in the side hall opened and closed, and a woman in her late sixties or early seventies emerged pushing a trolley stacked with boxes.

At the sight of him, her eyes widened beneath gray-fringed bangs. "Oh, I didn't hear you come in. You been waitin' long?"

"No, ma'am." He went closer but kept a respectable distance. "Want help with those boxes—" he glanced at her nametag, "Rita? They look heavy."

When she got a better look at him—scrapes, bruises and grime—wariness wrinkled her brow. "No, thank you. I may be small, but I'm tough."

He lifted his hands, palms up, and stepped back. "I understand. Sorry about my appearance. My girlfriend and I were at a party and were robbed. They took everything. Our wallets. Phones. We've been walking for miles." Gesturing over his shoulder, he said, "I was wondering if I could possibly use the phone to call a friend of mine for a ride."

She tilted her head and contemplated him for long, tense seconds. Did she recognize him?

Finally, she jammed her hands on her hips. "People these days have no respect for hard work. They wanna live the easy life and take what doesn't belong to them."

"Unfortunately, that's true for some."

"Just last week, my grandson's riding mower was taken from his garage, while he was in the back weedeating. Can you believe that?"

"Terrible."

She peered around. "Where's your girlfriend?"

"In the bathroom washing up."

Bustling past him, she said, "Come on up and use the phone."

"Thank you. I appreciate it, ma'am."

She extended the receiver across the counter. "You know, you look awfully familiar. You live around here?"

His heart tripped. "No, ma'am. Near the base."

"You're a marine? My late husband did a four-year stint in the Marines. Dearest Thomas. He was my soul mate."

Julian worked to keep his impatience at bay. "I'm sorry for your loss."

Her eyes misted. "I miss him. House ain't the same without him." Her gaze shifted beyond his shoulder. "Oh, my dear! Aren't you a pitiful sight!"

Turning, he saw Audrey coming up the center aisle. She'd washed her face and hands and finger-combed her long hair, but her makeup-free skin was as white as a fresh blanket of snow. Her blue eyes looked bigger and darker than usual and were full of caution. There was no hiding the scratches on her throat.

"Um, thank you for the use of your bathroom facilities," she said, her gaze lingering on Julian.

"Of course, dear." The cashier released the phone to his possession and, going around to where Audrey stood, took her hands. "You must be traumatized by your ordeal. Horrible, black-hearted thieves."

"Well, I—"

"I want you to help yourself to a cup of coffee."

Her mouth rounded. "Oh, but I don't have—"

"Any money? I know. Your fella told me. Come on, let's get you something to drink. Grab a biscuit, too. The manager lets me take home what we don't sell, which is usually a sackful."

Swallowing the lump in his throat, Julian dialed Brady's number. He answered on the third ring.

"Captain Johnson."

"Brady, it's Tan. Listen, a friend and I could use your help."

"Is this friend a nurse named Audrey Harris?"

He'd seen the news. "That's the one. I'll explain when you get here."

"What all do you need?"

"Cash. Nonperishable food. A place to crash."

"You don't ask for much, do you?" He sighed. "What's your location?"

Julian read the address off the phone. Through the large panes of glass, he saw a truck pull alongside the pumps. A man in overalls emerged and rambled toward the entrance.

"We'll be around back. Hurry, Brady."

"Will do."

The man patted his pockets, did a three-sixty and returned to the truck, probably to retrieve his wallet. A brief reprieve.

Hurrying over to where Rita was chatting up Audrey, he said, "Sorry to interrupt, but we have to go outside and wait for our friend. He's in a rush to get to work. Thank you for the use of the phone."

"And for the coffee," Audrey added.

Rita was stuffing a variety of biscuit sandwiches into a brown paper bag. "I don't want you two dears to go hungry."

Over his shoulder, Julian could see the man in overalls approaching. If he sounded the alarm, they'd have to make a run for it. Their rendezvous with Brady would be toast.

He tapped his foot and resisted the urge to snatch the bag from her grip.

Her freckled hands were slowly rolling the paper closed. "Don't you want a coffee, too?"

"That's okay." Clasping Audrey's hand, he said, "Audrey doesn't mind sharing, do you, sweetheart?"

"Not at all."

She handed him the foam cup. He took a sip and pretended to like the bitter brew.

The door hinges squeaked on the other side of the store. Julian tensed. Audrey sucked in a breath before ducking her head.

The man clomped down the aisle and headed for the restrooms.

Thank You, Lord.

He began edging Audrey toward the exit. "Have a great day, ma'am."

She pressed the bag into Audrey's free hand. "You take care."

Once outside, Julian hustled her along the exterior wall and around to the back. He surveyed the area and decided that the best place to hunker down would be behind the oversize garbage container.

Audrey clutched the bag to her chest. Lines of strain bracketed her mouth. "Is your friend coming?"

"Yes."

Positioned at the container's edge, he had a clear view of the road. Another vehicle pulled in. They'd timed it just right. He hoped Brady picked them up before Rita realized her television was turned off. Or before a chatty customer filled her in.

"Does he know we're in trouble?"

His grip tightened on the cup. Holding it out to her, he said, "Brady saw the report but agreed to help without knowing the particulars."

She sipped the stout brew. Above the rim, he could see the dip between her eyebrows.

"Captain Johnson is *'ohana*. Family. He'll do whatever he can for us."

"I don't recognize his name. Is he force recon?"

"He's with the 269 Squadron, the Gunrunners. He's a pilot." He resumed scanning the road, then said, "Brady was supposed to pilot the bird the day it went down. He was grounded due to a migraine."

"I suppose he shares the same misplaced guilt you do."

"Maybe."

They hadn't discussed it. Brady had been in a bad head space for a while now, thanks to the unexpected death of his best friend and fellow pilot. The accident had no doubt heaped more stress on him. Julian hadn't bothered to ask how he was doing because he'd been too inward-focused. Shame bit at him.

Shaking off the thoughts, he took note of her silence and saw that she was sipping her coffee and staring at nothing.

"Why don't you have a seat and eat something?"

"I can't stop thinking about everyone I know waking up and seeing the notifications about a dangerous couple on the loose." Her throat worked. "My bosses and coworkers. My church family. My dad."

He framed her face with both hands and gazed down into her tormented eyes. "The people who know and love you won't believe what the media is saying."

Her lower lip trembled, and he longed to caress it. "You were right. I should've told my dad from the start. The confusion and worry he must be experiencing right now..." A single tear slipped down her cheek. "The shame and scrutiny. He's probably getting grilled by the police right this second. He'll find out what's been happening at the hospital, and deep inside, he'll wonder if he misjudged me. He'll wonder if I got into drugs or—or the wrong crowd..."

Julian's heart threatened to split in two. Her sadness weighed on him, made him feel helpless. He put his arms around her and, tucking her head against his chest, held her close.

"Things will get sorted out. We have the truth on our side."

"You promise?"

In response, he placed a light kiss against her hair. "I'm going to take care of you to the best of my ability, Audrey. I promise you that."

He felt her shudder, and her weight rested more fully against him. She was soft curves and silken skin. He would've gladly held her all day, but the sound of a rumbling engine approaching reminded him to be on guard.

Easing away, he shifted closer to the container and recognized the sedan. Relief washed over him.

"Our ride's here."

When Audrey hung back, he held out his hand. "It's okay, sweetheart. You don't have to be afraid."

"I'm tired, Julian."

"We'll rest soon."

"I—I think I—" The bag dropped to the ground, and she sank to her knees.

Julian sprang to her side in the grass and, one arm supporting her back, took the cup from her grip. "Audrey, talk to me."

She opened her mouth to speak, but no sound came out. Her head went slack, and she fainted in his arms.

FOURTEEN

"**D**oes she have any preexisting conditions?"

"She hasn't mentioned any." Someone reverently stroked her hair. "She hasn't had anything to eat in hours and zero sleep."

"That could do it."

Concerned male voices roused Audrey. A thick, comfy blanket supported her head, and heat from car vents soothed her chilled skin. Her eyes blinked open, and she realized Julian was her pillow.

She sat up too quickly, and black dots started dancing in her vision again.

"Hey." Julian cupped her nape. "Put your head down and breathe."

"I don't have health issues," she said, focusing on the reassuring weight of his hand beneath her hair.

She breathed in and out, filling her lungs with the scents of leather, cologne and male. The driver, whom she'd yet to meet, kept the car at a steady, sedate pace, for which she was thankful.

"As soon as the dizziness passes, I want you to eat one of those biscuits Rita gave you."

"Okay."

Julian started tracing patterns on her skin—a definite distraction from her cotton-filled head.

"Brady, how far out are we?"

"Twenty minutes. My uncle has a vacant storefront in Jacksonville's downtown area. There's a kitchenette and bathroom with shower upstairs. The power's on, so you'll have electricity and hot water."

"Downtown consists of a couple of streets," Julian mused. "Not a lot of area to blend in."

"It's the only place I could come up with on short notice. It's been vacant for almost a year. There are several buildings standing empty. As long as you're discreet, you should be okay."

"I know we've asked a lot of you, brother. I'm grateful."

Audrey slowly straightened and met the driver's gaze in the rearview mirror. "Hi. I'm Audrey."

Curiosity swirled in the blue-gray depths. "Hello, Audrey." Offering her a bottled water over the seat, he said, "You feeling better?"

"A little."

Julian—who'd donned a black baseball cap—set the sack on her lap. "Start eating."

She gave it back. "You first."

Brady coughed to cover a laugh. From her vantage point, she could see that he had a strong profile, short blond hair and a surfer tan.

Julian waited until she'd started on her sausage biscuit before unwrapping his own. He downed it in four bites and, after chugging half his water bottle, relayed the events that had led to them reaching out to the captain.

"Incredible." Brady's grip on the wheel held steady as he drove them deeper into the city. "I had no idea Jacksonville had an organized-crime problem."

"My gut tells me this isn't a singular operation, but a small part of a state-wide network. Gerald's operation is too sophisticated. He'd need cash flow from more than one modest military town."

Brady sucked in air. "Cruiser incoming."

Julian's arm came around her. Audrey leaned into his side and buried her face in his chest. He rested his cheek atop her hair. The hat's bill effectively hid his features. Beneath her cheek, his heart thrummed strong and steady. She didn't want to leave the haven of his arms. She wanted to belong there. She wanted to be his partner, his actual girlfriend.

But she wasn't. Nor would she be.

"He's gone."

Reluctantly, she returned to her side of the bench seat. Julian didn't look in her direction, and his expression didn't give any hints to what he was feeling. Probably nothing. This was a mission of survival, and he was a professional. A trained marine who'd likely been taught to shut down his emotions in order to achieve his goals.

If they were fortunate enough to return to their former lives, he'd probably be happy to be rid of her. That offer to cook for her? Careless words spoken without forethought.

By the time Brady parked the car behind an old brick building, Audrey was feeling glum and out of sorts. Glancing along the strip of pavement stretching behind the row of old buildings, she reminded herself that Julian's lack of feelings for her shouldn't matter. Their lives were at stake.

Sleep would restore her common sense, she hoped. Her eyes were gritty, and she still felt disoriented.

They waited in the car while Brady unlocked the back door and carried in two cardboard boxes. There was no sign of activity. Because it was Sunday, most of the downtown shops were closed. That would work to their advantage.

He gave the signal. Julian grabbed a pair of camouflage sleeping bags from the front seat and, together, they hurried inside.

"That's a combination storage closet and office," Brady said, pointing to a room on their right. "This door opposite hides a utility closet."

He led them into a large, open space with exposed brick

walls and solid plank floors. An antique chandelier gave it an air of old-world elegance.

"What type of business was this?" she asked, examining one of the dangling crystals.

"The building dates back to the late nineteenth century." He shifted the boxes in his arms. "I've heard it was once a nursing school and later an insurance office. My aunt and uncle purchased it before I was born and opened an upscale clothing store. Aunt Donna passed a decade ago, and none of their children were interested in continuing the business. He's rented it out to various clients, but nothing has ever stuck."

At the front, twin plate-glass windows flanked the main door. Cardboard covered the windows, but not the tall, narrow glass inserts on either side of the door. They'd have to remain on guard against curious passersby.

Walking between two half walls, they passed the main entrance and proceeded to a steep staircase tucked between Sheetrock and brick.

"Watch your step," he warned, going first.

Audrey ascended after him, and Julian brought up the rear. The upstairs was slightly warmer than the first floor. Julian must've noticed her shiver, because he asked Brady about adjusting the thermostat. There were multiple rooms off either side of the hallway, occupied with the odd cushioned chair and plenty of cobwebs. The promised kitchenette was at the rear of the house, overlooking the patchy woods that separated the commercial property and a decent-size church and grounds.

Brady deposited the boxes on the floor and closed the window blinds. The morning sunlight stole in around the blinds' borders, preventing the room from being too dark.

"As you can see, it's not exactly what you'd call a luxury kitchen."

Chipped Formica counters topped white cabinets. The microwave and cooktop were old but clean. He tested the sink faucet.

"There's no dining table," he added, stroking his chin.

"We'll sit on the floor," she said, overwhelmed by this stranger's generosity. The captain was taking a huge risk. "In my profession, you become used to microwave meals."

Brady nodded. "I'd stick around, but I've got to hustle out to the air station. They called for a surprise briefing."

Julian clasped his friend's upper arm. "I owe you, brother."

"You'd do the same for me," he insisted. Patting his pocket, he said, "The officer's phone will hopefully contain incriminating information."

"Take care it can't be traced to your location."

"Understood. I'll be back tonight."

When he'd gone, they sorted through the boxes and found toothbrushes, toothpaste and assorted toiletries. There were a variety of canned foods, snacks and bottles of water. He'd even thought to include washcloths and towels.

Her eyes smarted. "I pray Brady doesn't get in trouble for helping us."

"We have to think positive," he said, removing his hat and running his fingers through the thatch of brown-black hair. "Now, would you rather shower or sleep first?"

"Shower first, then sleep."

"Roger."

After Audrey showered and scrubbed her teeth in the tiny, claustrophobic bathroom, she discovered Julian unrolling a sleeping bag near the kitchenette. He placed the thick blanket he'd had in the car at the top.

"This will have to do for a pillow," he said. Getting to his feet, he took in her wrinkled, dirty clothes and damp, combed hair hanging about her shoulders. "We'll get changes of clothes soon."

How they would manage that and how long they'd have to hide out here were things she didn't want to contemplate. Right now, she craved dreamless, peaceful sleep. The hot water had massaged her sore muscles and left her deliriously sleepy.

He tucked the other sleeping bag beneath his arm. "I'm going to crash downstairs."

"What if someone sees you?"

"No one will see me. I'll stay hidden behind the half wall." His gaze held hers. "Sweet dreams, Audrey."

She watched him disappear down the stairs, then crawled into her makeshift pallet. His scent clung to the soft blanket. Gazing up at the ceiling, Audrey prayed the feelings bursting to life in her heart would leave her.

A car horn woke her midafternoon. She didn't wear a watch, and without a phone, she couldn't be sure of the exact time. The building was silent. Tiptoeing down the stairs, she peeked over the half wall and discovered Julian sitting against the brick, his eyes closed and his arms resting on his bent knees.

His hair was damp, the longer strands on top slightly mussed. He must've washed up while she was sleeping.

Without opening his eyes, he spoke. "Get any sleep?"

She startled. "Um, yes, I did. Surprisingly, I fell asleep within minutes." Easing around the partition and taking a seat beside him, she smelled shaving soap and noticed the hint of dark whiskers was gone. "Did you?"

"A little." Turning his head in her direction, he stared deeply into her eyes. The tawny depths held a host of mysteries she would dearly like to unravel.

"What are you thinking about?" she said.

His lids swept down, and he rubbed at the crease on his black pant leg. "My family."

"You're hoping they don't get wind of this."

"It would confirm for my father that I made the wrong choice," he said, shrugging. "That he was right, and I should've gone into law, like him."

She found it difficult to grasp how anyone could fail to admire Julian's commitment, dedication and self-sacrifice. He put his own life in jeopardy in order to protect their country. "If I had a chance to talk to your father, I could extol your virtues for hours. Maybe days."

His head was bent down, but she glimpsed his half smile. "Days, huh?"

"Yes, days." Putting her hand on his shoulder, she leaned in. "You're the best man I know."

He shifted in her direction and pressed his palm to her forehead. "You sure you aren't running a fever, Nurse Harris?"

His teasing tone was at odds with the intensity of his direct gaze.

"I should rephrase that to say that you and my dad are the best men I know. He wouldn't be happy to be left out."

His brows buckled, and he lowered his hand. "*Mahalo*, Audrey."

"Don't let your father's disapproval diminish what you've accomplished. And remember, no matter what our earthly father is like, we have a Heavenly Father who loves and cherishes us."

"It is amazing. To think a holy, perfect God, who created us and knows our failures, still seeks a relationship with us."

"His love for us mirrors the parent-child relationship. According to my dad, a child can make foolish, infuriating choices and yet she can't shake a dad's unconditional love."

Remembering Trent's exasperation when he'd said that to her on the many occasions she'd messed up, she chuckled.

Julian's attention sharpened, and she felt a charge in the air. He curved his big, warm hand around her cheek and captured her lips with his. She didn't move. Didn't breathe. Just basked in the sweetness of his kiss. The rightness of it.

He paused. Lifted his head.

"Why did you do that?" she whispered.

"Your smile. It's like snow in Hawaii—a rare occurrence." He stroked his thumb over her cheekbone. "Are you angry?"

Trembling inside, she cupped the back of his head and brought his lips to hers once more.

Julian ignored the warning siren in his head. Audrey was too precious—an unexpected treasure he'd never thought to search for. Holding her, savoring her tender caresses, fractured the dam holding his emotions at bay. He'd gone weak. Her brilliant smile, that joyous laugh bubbling up from her throat, had galvanized him. Blasted his previous decision to keep their relationship platonic. And, oh, the way her blue eyes had betrayed her, glistening with affection and possibly more when she'd said what she'd said.

You're the best man I know.

Coming from a woman like Audrey, the assertion both thrilled and humbled him.

He lifted his head, pulled her close and simply held her. Her hair tickled his chin, and her soft breath fanned over his throat. He'd never felt this profound connection with anyone else. He hadn't let himself. It shook him. Frightened him more than anything he'd faced in enemy territory. This was her heart on the line. Hers and his.

Being with her wasn't an option. Julian had shied away from commitment to the point that it had become a habit.

Chin and Layla Tan had achieved marital satisfaction that he couldn't hope to replicate.

Or maybe that's a handy excuse you've crafted to hide the fact you're scared to try and fail.

Her stomach rumbled.

Laughing, she pulled away. "I suppose it's time to go upstairs and heat up lunch. I hope Brady remembered a can opener."

Her eyes were bright, her cheeks pink, and her mouth curved in a shy smile. Her long tresses curled around her shoulders and were frizzy from lack of gel or mousse or whatever she used. No makeup to enhance her eyes or cheekbones. And her clothes were ready for the burn pile.

Julian had never seen a more beautiful woman in all his life.

Standing to his feet, he held out his hand and helped her up. He rolled up his sleeping bag and followed her upstairs, his thoughts a muddle. He should regret kissing her, but he couldn't.

It was important they don't get distracted, however. He waited until she'd finished her soup to broach an unpleasant reality.

"When I don't report for duty in the morning, I'll be considered AWOL."

Her spoon and bowl clattered in the sink. Whirling, she sagged against the counter. "Oh, Julian. I didn't even consider that."

"Everything will be sorted in the end," he said, trying not to heap more worry on her. But he was worried himself. What if this episode affected the Marine Corps's decision about his future?

He carried his own bowl over and rinsed out both of them. "We'll have to be extra careful tonight."

Once the corps got their hands on him, he and Audrey

would be separated. He'd go to the base brig and she'd be shuttled off to the civilian police, where Officer Craddock could dispense his own twisted justice. He couldn't let that happen.

"What's tonight?" Audrey asked. "We aren't staying here?"

"If we don't root out the truth, who will? Not Craddock or Dunn. With the suspicion on us, the other detectives might consider the case closed. We have to find out who at Onslow General is playing puppet for Gerald."

"How do we do that when we're stuck here?"

"Brady promised to arrange for a vehicle and a couple of burner phones." He laid the dishes out to dry. "First stop? Frank Russo's."

Her brows shot up. "Frank is your prime suspect?"

"He resents you, Audrey. That much is obvious. He also has the physical signs of a user."

With her hip tucked against the cabinet and her fingers tapping on the Formica, she studied him. "Frank isn't on the top of your list, though, is he?"

His jaw sagged. How had she guessed?

"Who is it?" she persisted.

"Chasity. Or Lincoln. Maybe both."

Denial sparked to life in her eyes. "I can't believe that."

"That's why I haven't mentioned it."

It wasn't the only reason. From the start, he'd been overly protective of her. He'd do anything to avoid hurting her, but now he wondered if keeping this to himself had been the right thing. Because she was looking at him as if they suddenly weren't on the same team anymore.

"What on earth would make you suspect my friends?"

FIFTEEN

At the sight of Julian's unhappy expression, Audrey tamped down her outrage.

He wouldn't be a very good protector if he didn't consider all the angles. But he was wrong.

"Chasity and I were roommates in college. We bonded over clinicals and final exams. We've worked in the same hospital for a long time. First of all, she would never do anything to hurt me. Secondly, she loves her job and is committed to her patients' well-being." The idea that Chasity would willingly agree to work for a criminal was ludicrous.

"Some people are masters at hiding parts of themselves from those they are closest to. I've read about it in news articles and seen it played out in real life." He pinched the bridge of his nose. "We can't rule out anyone on your list, starting with those you interact with most. Think, Audrey. Are there any red flags? Has Chasity's behavior or habits changed in the last year? The last six months?"

"No. There's nothing of note. About a year ago, she had a brief relationship with a rookie police officer. Not long after, she and Lincoln started dating. Honestly, she's the happiest I've ever seen her."

Audrey thought back to the party. Had it been less than twenty-four hours? It felt like a lifetime. Chasity's eyes had been as bright and sparkly as the rock on her finger.

"I had reservations about her dating Lincoln," she said.

"Because he was a rebound relationship?"

She shook her head. "The officer thing was very casual. A couple of movies and dinner dates. Lincoln, as you probably gathered, is popular among the female employees. He's handsome, charming and successful. I was afraid Chasity would get her heart broken." Shrugging, she swept her hair forward and began plaiting it. "But he's devoted to her. I've no doubt he'd move heaven and earth for her."

Julian seemed to consider her words, his gaze tracking the movement of her fingers. The memory of their closeness made her heart feel full of that sizzling, popping candy she used to eat as a kid. His touch was forever seared on her soul. She wouldn't take it back if she could, despite the near certainty that she wouldn't emerge from this unscathed.

He dragged his gaze to hers. "Were you also concerned about his divorce? I got the sense it wasn't amicable."

"From what I've gathered, Gina's only goal was to accumulate more wealth and greater social status. Jacksonville, and Lincoln, hindered those goals."

"Has he complained about spousal support?"

"Not that I know of. Why?"

The sound of the downstairs door opening brought the conversation to a halt. Julian put his fingers to his lips. Peeking through the window, he shook his head to indicate he didn't recognize the vehicle. Or maybe there wasn't one. He moved stealthily to the top of the stairs, all six-two of him taut and ready to pounce.

Audrey started to follow. He stopped her with a single, stay-put glance.

Purposeful footsteps echoed in the empty space below. Coming closer.

Adrenaline pumped through her system. There would be no flight in this situation. Stay and fight.

"Tan? You up there?"

Beneath Julian's white cotton shirt, his rigid shoulders bunched and relaxed. "McMann?"

Audrey couldn't resist joining Julian. A raven-haired man appeared at the bottom, his assessing blue gaze bouncing between them. Based on his military regulation haircut, straight-spine stance and air of command, she guessed he was a marine.

"What are you doing here?" Julian demanded. "I could've put a bullet in you, and then Tori would've throttled me."

He dangled a set of keys and began the climb. "I was told you could use a ride."

They moved farther down the hallway to give him room.

"Audrey, this is Cade McMann. He's a staff sergeant with a grunt unit at Lejeune." His brow furrowed. "I thought you and Tori would be in California by now."

"Our move date got pushed back two months." Handing Julian the keys, he looked at Audrey. "It's nice to meet you, Audrey. I wish it was under better circumstances."

His expression was sincere. Kind, even. Still, she couldn't help wondering if Julian's friends blamed her for putting him in harm's way. "Me, too."

Julian led them into the dining and kitchenette area. "Brady shouldn't have involved you. Too risky."

"You were there for Tori and me when we were in trouble. Of course I want to be involved. I'll do whatever you need me to."

Julian set his chin in that familiar stubborn angle. "Tori is exactly why you should stay out of it."

"She'd be appalled if I didn't help. In fact, she insisted you borrow her car."

Audrey separated the blinds slats. A black Volkswagen Beetle was parked parallel to the building.

Julian arched an eyebrow. "The car you bought to replace the one that got blown up?"

"Excuse me?" Audrey turned away from the window.

Cade grimaced. "It's a complicated story."

"Like ours?" she said.

"Yes." He nodded, his expression grave. "But we survived. God walked us through it, just like He will you and Julian."

"What's your plan?"

Julian's gaze lingered on Audrey and Brady, who were talking in the opposite corner near the bathroom. The captain had arrived shortly after Cade, bearing more gifts. A change of clothes for each of them—purchased at the base exchange—and pillows and burner phones.

"Tan?"

"Hmm?" Forcing his attention to Cade, he noticed the perceptive smile and knew he'd been caught. "What did you say?"

"I asked about your plans, but maybe I should be asking a different question."

"You can ask. Doesn't mean I'll answer," he retorted. "As for finding a way out of this predicament, we're going to have to perform our own detective work. Learning the identity of the person who framed Audrey is key." He told Cade about Frank, Chasity and Lincoln. "There's also her supervisor to consider—Veronica Mills."

"Let me come with you. Audrey can stay here." Shoving his hands in his pockets, he said, "Brady has no one to go home to. He'd agree to keep her company."

That was true. Brady had no family—his parents had abandoned him as a child, and the grandmother who'd raised him had already passed. Because of his troubled childhood, the pilot was very selective about who he let close. He didn't date often. Most assumed he was married to his career, but Julian thought Brady was simply scared of getting hurt.

"Audrey won't agree to stay behind and be babysat."

"She doesn't look tough," Cade said softly. "In fact, she gives off a feminine, fragile vibe."

Julian bristled. "You're dead wrong. She's got courage in spades. If you'd seen her in action like I have—rushing in to save both of us despite her lack of training—you wouldn't spout such nonsense."

Grinning, Cade gripped his arm. "Relax, brother. You know others frequently underestimate my wife, as well, to their peril."

Unclenching his fists, he rolled his eyes. Cade was fishing for information Julian wasn't about to divulge, goading him to reveal his feelings.

"Why don't you go home to her, McMann?"

"Evasive. Defensive. You've got the classic signs." Cade's grin turned wolfish. "Wait until Tori hears this."

"Hears what?" Brady said, strolling over.

He and Audrey had abandoned their corner and were looking at them with undisguised interest.

"Nothing." Julian shot Cade a quelling glance.

In truth, he wasn't so much irritated with his friend as he was with himself. He was supposed to be adept at keeping his thoughts and emotions hidden. It had only taken Cade minutes to figure out the score. If this work hiatus continued much longer, he'd have to repeat his training. And the SERE program, where certain government personnel went to learn survival skills, had hardly been a walk in the park.

After the men left, Audrey grabbed the plastic bag Brady had given her. "I'm going to change."

"Hold on a minute." Julian rifled through his bag and

produced a small box. "I asked Brady to get you some-thing."

Her nose wrinkled in distaste. "You want me to dye my hair?"

"A hat and dark glasses are enough to disguise me. I'm going to forgo shaving for a while and—" He produced a pair of cut-outs—a large, black scorpion and a simple anchor. "Sport temporary tattoos."

She came over and inspected them. "Those look real."

"It's tattoo paper. Brady printed them using a home printer. I'll need you to wet the adhesive and apply the let-ters." He indicated the area on the back of his neck above his collar. "The scorpion will go on my biceps where it will be visible beneath my T-shirt."

Her eyes were big and dark, her face inches from his. Memories of their recent kiss, as well as the many emo-tionally charged moments they'd shared, surged, an intan-gible but powerful connection. He wasn't alone in what was developing between them, and that made it harder to fight.

Clearing her throat, she curved her hair behind her ear. "I can handle that."

"I don't have tattoos, so this should cause any casual suspicions to be dismissed upon first glance."

"Right." Flipping over the dye box, she skimmed the directions. Straight, white teeth worried her bottom lip.

"It's your decision," he said.

"Oh, why not? I might decide I like it."

Julian parked the Volkswagen several houses down from Frank's. He lived in an older section of town, which was a mixture of restored bungalows with neat lawns and run-down homes with cracked driveways and chain-link fencing. Frank's belonged to the latter group. A broken streetlight aided their task—they could slip into his yard undetected and break in.

"Do you know if he has a dog?" Julian asked, his hand at her elbow.

"No pets. He's allergic."

"Good."

"What do we do if he comes home?"

"We have a chat with him."

Pulse racing, Audrey entered through the gate he held open. Together, they strode through the carport and around to the back. Shoulder-high hedges rimmed the modest yard. A dilapidated shed sat at a steep angle in the far corner. The house was cloaked in complete darkness.

Julian jimmied the rear door open and entered first, passing his flashlight over the interior. "Kitchen."

An odd odor assailed her. "Smells like marijuana." Sensing his surprise, she said, "Enough patients come in with the stench on their clothes. I haven't noticed it on Frank. He probably stores his scrubs in a locker at work."

"Let's start in the master bedroom."

Audrey stayed close behind him. The old floors creaked and groaned with their weight, and she hoped the joists didn't give way.

"If Frank is getting paid on the side," she said, "he isn't funneling the money into the upkeep of his home."

"Could be building a nest egg," Julian said, striding into the bedroom and bouncing the beam around. "Or fueling a drug addiction."

"Gerald doesn't strike me as the type to suffer fools. He wouldn't put up with a drugged-out RN for long."

"Good point. They'd be at risk of leaking his secret, too."

While he searched under and around the bed, Audrey flicked on her own flashlight and rummaged through the chest of drawers. Nothing of interest there. She went into the grimy bathroom and, tamping down her disgust, looked through the drawers and under the sink. She even lifted the lid of the toilet tank to be sure he hadn't strapped something to the inside. Gross.

Returning to the room and wishing she had sanitizer gel, she found Julian rifling through the closet. A single lightbulb swinging from a string cast a circle of light on the contents and him. She caught the way he glanced at her. His enigmatic gaze ran over her hair and, predictably, his lips firmed into a tight line. This particular reaction had played out multiple times ever since she'd adopted her new hair color... Ruby Rush.

She lifted her fingers to her loose braid. "You hate it, don't you?"

"No," he sighed. "I do not hate it."

"Well, I don't like your tattoos."

His brows inched up a notch.

Twin beams strobed through the bedroom window as a car pulled into the driveway. Julian tugged on the lightbulb string, and darkness blanketed the room.

Audrey forgot to be upset as he positioned himself at the window. "Frank's getting out of the car." Julian muttered beneath his breath. "He's got company."

"What?" Clutching his shoulder, she leaned closer to the glass and spotted three men exiting a truck that was blocking Frank's driveway. "Maybe we should sneak out the back."

"Hold on."

Frank lifted his hands, palms up, and his mouth started flapping. Two men flanked him and the third got up close and personal.

"They don't look anything like Gerald's men," she said.

These were street thugs as opposed to high-class goons-for-hire.

"Whoever they are, they aren't happy to see him."

Julian shifted his stance, and his cheek brushed her temple.

She unpeeled her fingers from his muscular physique. "Sorry. Didn't mean to crowd you."

"I wasn't bothered," he said, shrugging.

Audrey would've liked to discuss what was happening between them. He was the first man she'd allowed herself to care about since losing Seth. Not that she'd consciously chosen to like him. The feelings had taken root as they'd been thrown together in one dangerous situation after another. If only Julian wasn't skilled at pulling a curtain over his feelings, maybe she'd have a clue how he felt about her. Was he happy about that kiss? Or did he regret it? Did he like her as much as she liked him?

Was he—like her—trying to remain levelheaded about the whole thing and not let it get out of control?

Audrey was relieved he couldn't read her thoughts. This was hardly the time for self-examination.

Outside, Frank was gesturing wildly and nodding his head. Whatever he said convinced them to leave. Their tires squealed as they rumbled down the street.

"Let's go."

Julian hustled her to the laundry room off the kitchen. He told her to stay there until he was certain Frank wasn't armed. Without his own weapon, Julian had to use brute force and cunning to subdue the enemy.

She didn't do exactly as instructed. Flattened against the hulking fridge just outside the laundry room, she inched farther into the kitchen and was able to discern Julian's tall form wedged in the corner behind the door.

Frank rushed inside, locked the door behind him and switched on the overhead light. He tossed his keys on the round dining table and buried his face in his hands.

Julian left his hiding spot. "Hello, Frank."

Frank gasped and whipped around. "Who are you?" He shoved a chair between them. "What are you doing in my house?"

"Who were those men, Frank?" Julian advanced.

"I've seen you before. Where?" His retreat brought him closer to Audrey. "I—I'm going to call the cops."

"I don't think you want to do that." His steps were slow. Measured. "You're involved in something shady, aren't you, Frank?"

He lunged for the knife block beside the sink and brandished a long, sharp blade. "Get out."

Julian cocked a single brow.

Audrey stepped fully into the room. "Drop the knife, Frank."

Frank's mouth slackened. "What have you done to your hair?" Then his brows snapped together. Dislike oozed from his pores. "Now I'm calling the cops. Two fugitives have invaded my home."

The moment he sank his free hand in his jeans pocket, Julian snapped into action—he relieved Frank of his weapon, imprisoned his arm behind his back and shoved him into the nearest wooden chair.

Audrey picked up the discarded knife and replaced it in the block. Turning back, she caught his baleful glare and suppressed a shudder. Now that she'd been ousted from the hospital, he wasn't attempting to mask his loathing.

"You've been nothing but trouble since you transferred to our unit," he spat.

Julian's grip on the back of his neck intensified. "Because she interfered with your operation, right? She didn't turn a blind eye on your illegal activities. Pretty inconvenient for you and your friends, I'd say."

A vein bulged in his temple. "No. I didn't have anything to do with the missing supplies or diverted narcotics. Everyone believes she's the culprit," he sneered. "If it looks like a duck and walks like a duck..."

Audrey's spirits sagged. She'd feared that would be the outcome of the news report.

Julian's lips thinned. Bringing his mouth close to Frank's ear, he spoke with soft, deadly promise. "I've been taught how to kill a man with my bare hands. It's easier than you might think."

The color drained from his face. "I can't help you."

"You can and you will, starting with the identity of those men and what they want with you."

Jaw hardening, he squirmed on the chair, his bloodshot eyes shifting from side to side.

"Audrey, please go in the other room," Julian said.

His shuttered expression revealed nothing of his intentions.

She hesitated, rocking back on her feet.

He lifted his coppery brown eyes. "I don't want you to have to witness this."

Frank cranked his head around. "Witness what?"

"Audrey." A muscle twitched in his cheek.

Was he serious? "I've been exposed to plenty of unpleasant sights in my line of work."

"If you stay and watch," he uttered calmly, "you could be called to testify against me."

Something flashed in his eyes. "Oh." She started to leave.

"Wait!" Frank called out. "Ronald's my bookie. The other two are higher up the gambling chain."

Julian scowled. "Illegal gambling, Frank? You expect me to believe that?"

"It's the truth." Sweat beaded his upper lip. "I can prove it."

He cracked his knuckles. "I'm waiting."

"Behind the dryer. There's a metal box."

Audrey returned to the laundry room. "Found it."

Scooting the dryer a few centimeters out from the wall enabled her to retrieve the box. She set it on the dining table and pried open the lid. Stacks of bills, along with gambling stats on everything from MMA fights to horse races to basketball games, supported his claim.

"You see?"

Julian thumbed through the notebooks. "You've had more slumps than wins lately."

"My fortunes will turn around."

"Better rethink that before you get yourself killed."

Taking out his burner phone, he snapped pictures of Frank holding the box of evidence, as well as up-close photos of the stats in his handwriting. He stuffed one notepad into his cargo pants' side pocket. "If, after we leave here, you contact the authorities or tell anyone about our visit, these will wind up in a detective's inbox. Understand?"

His Adam's apple bobbed. "I won't snitch."

When they were in the car driving away, she turned to stare out the rear window. It had been strange to see gruff, belligerent Frank trembling with fear.

"Do you think he'll keep his word?" she said, turning to face forward.

Julian was as unflappable as ever. "He's the type to protect his own interests above everything else. He won't risk it."

Her gaze traced his profile as passing streetlights threw it in sharp relief. "Were you bluffing? Threatening him to get him to talk?"

One hand held the wheel, the other rested on his thigh. "The goal is always to achieve my objectives without the use of violence."

"Unless you have no other choice."

"I'm a force-recon marine, Audrey. It's not what I *do*. It's who I *am*."

The statement wasn't new. As the daughter of a marine, she'd heard similar slogans. *Once a marine, always a marine.* Julian's passion set him apart. He loved the corps. He lived and breathed a warrior's life. It was a timely reminder to focus on what was important—clearing their names and putting Gerald and his cohorts behind bars.

There was no room in his life for her.

When they passed into a more populated area, she scooted lower in the seat.

A gentle tug on her braid brought her attention back to Julian.

"For the record, I'm a fan of red."

"You're just saying that."

"The truth is, I thought you couldn't be anymore beautiful than you already are." His liquid gaze had gone soft, a warm caress as tangible as a touch. "I was wrong."

She steeled herself against the delight fizzing and popping inside. "I still don't like your tattoos."

SIXTEEN

Something was troubling Audrey.

Julian would've liked to assign it to their circumstances, but he sensed it had more to do with the emotional element underscoring their every exchange.

He sighed. "That kiss—"

"A mistake," she said, shaking her head. "A reckless moment."

Her words of dismissal cut into him. His rational self applauded her evaluation. His heart, long insulated and guarded, quailed.

Staring straight ahead, he kept his expression neutral and his grip on the wheel slack.

"Seriously, what were we thinking?" She waved her hand between them. "Nothing between us could possibly be real. It's manufactured emotion, that's all."

Julian couldn't speak past the tank-size lump in his throat. The silence doubled.

"Don't you agree?" she demanded.

How could he argue with her when everything he'd been taught about hostile operations supported her reasoning?

"Julian?"

He ground his teeth together. "Sure."

He drove down the mostly empty streets of Jacksonville. She rolled and unrolled the hem of her aquamarine long-sleeved cotton shirt. Although new, her jeans fit her like a soft glove. He applauded Brady's choice of sensible tennis shoes.

"Are we headed to the storefront?" Her words were stilted. Distant.

"If you've had enough sleuthing for one night, then yes."

"I'm not tired. We shouldn't waste time. The sooner we solve this puzzle and get the information to the police— someone in the department who isn't in league with Gerald—the sooner we can resume normal life."

He was starting to question whether that would be possible. Could they return to casual waves across the parking lot and the standard how-are-you? exchange in the elevator?

"We have two stops to make," he said.

"I won't invade Chasity's home and be part of an interrogation. I can't."

"I'll only go in if she's not home. It's twenty-two hundred hours. She could be out with friends."

"Or working a late shift. Sometimes she picks up extra."

Julian prayed that would be the case. Audrey's defense of her friends was natural and appropriate.

Following her directions, he drove to a tidy subdivision about a mile from the hospital. Chasity's modest, new construction rancher was in a cul-de-sac. Julian eased the car to the opposite curb and let it idle.

"Lights are on."

Audrey shifted forward in the seat. "She often leaves a couple on to discourage thieves."

He applied pressure to the gas pedal and started to follow the curve of the cul-de-sac.

"We're leaving?"

"I'm going to park in another section and hike back. If she's home, I'll try again tomorrow night."

Just as they were about to reach her house, the garage door opened. He hit the brakes.

"That's Lincoln's car," Audrey whispered. "Chasity's isn't there."

A low-slung silver Mercedes whipped out of the driveway in reverse, then shot out to the main street.

"Where's he off to so fast?"

"There's only one way to find out."

Julian tailed the surgeon through the neighborhood and onto the main highway, careful to remain far enough behind so as not to arouse suspicion. Even so, he had to exceed the speed limit in order to keep up. The last thing they needed was to draw attention for speeding.

When they zipped past the hospital, she said, "Guess he wasn't called in to perform an emergency surgery."

"Maybe it's his kids. I'm not driving an hour to Wilmington. We'll turn around if that's the direction he's headed." The longer they were on the streets, the higher the chance trouble might find them.

"He's not going home."

Lincoln had passed the turnoff that led to his upscale community and continued toward the waterfront. The surroundings became less residential and more commercial. Julian's gut hardened.

"Audrey, this is the way to the warehouses."

Her shoulders hunched. "I wouldn't remember."

Because she'd been bound and blinded. The terror he'd endured, not knowing her whereabouts or her condition, couldn't begin to match hers.

He lifted his foot from the gas.

"We're slowing down. Why?"

"I'm taking you back to the storefront."

She gripped his arm. "No, Julian. We can't afford to lose sight of him."

He glanced over at her. "He could be innocent."

"I'm holding out hope that he's taking a long route elsewhere, and that this is merely a coincidence."

"I don't want you anywhere near this place. I'm turning around."

"Julian, please."

An inner war ensued. Heed his instincts and get her as far away from Gerald as possible? Or accept that they were partners and respect her decision?

He resumed their previous speed. Too soon, Gerald's compound came into view, and the Mercedes made the turn. As they continued past the dead-end road, he glimpsed the rolling fence gate sliding open to admit Lincoln.

"I'm sorry."

"I never thought—" She audibly swallowed. "Lincoln's a good person. He's thoughtful and attentive and caring." Bowing her head, she covered her face with her hands.

Soon, her shock would wear off and anger would take its place.

He parked close to the same spot he'd used before. His own wasn't where he'd left it. The city had likely towed it. Or Gerald's men had gotten rid of it.

"I'll be back in five."

She clutched her door handle. "Where are you going?"

"To take a few pictures of Lincoln at this site. We have to have proof."

At this point, their reputations were in tatters and their word was worthless. A good police officer would believe a respected surgeon's denials over a couple accused of assaulting an officer.

"You're not going alone," she said.

"I need for you to stay here. In case I don't return, contact Brady."

"No—"

"We're running out of time to catch a glimpse of him outside."

Looking extremely displeased, she released the handle and pulled out her phone. "You have ten minutes, Sergeant."

"Yes, ma'am."

Closing the door and motioning for her to lock it, he jogged in the building's shadow until he reached the dead-end road. The entrance gate was directly across from him. With no cars or goons in sight, he dashed across the lanes.

Through the fencing, in the halo of exterior lights, he saw Lincoln running alongside the twins and barking orders. They were carrying a wounded man. He couldn't make out his identity or condition from this distance.

He took multiple pictures. When they entered the warehouse, he snapped another picture of the parking lot and Lincoln's Mercedes.

"Julian."

Audrey hadn't stayed in the car as promised. Opening his mouth to express his exasperation, he pivoted and everything inside him went cold.

"Phone, please." Josef kept the gun pointed at Audrey's head while motioning for Julian to toss his phone over.

Her eyes were huge with fear and regret. "I'm sorry."

His usual calm failing him, he let it clatter to the asphalt. "Let her go, and I'll lead you to the evidence we have on your boss."

"The Jungle King is untouchable. If you haven't learned that by now, you will."

Julian lunged. His forward motion was interrupted by a buzzing sound behind him. Electric volts vibrated through his body. His muscles convulsed, screaming in white-hot agony. He landed on the ground, helpless to stop Josef from dragging Audrey away.

"Where's Julian?" Audrey demanded, pitting her weight against Josef's forward march and making progress difficult. She didn't care about the gun he brandished. "I'll do whatever Gerald wants as long as he remains unharmed."

His grip on her arm turned bruising, and he hauled her through the warehouse doors. She couldn't hear or see Julian. That Taser blast had rendered him defenseless against the enemy. He was at their mercy again, and so was she.

At the wave of familiar moisture-laden air and the echo of macaw screams, she almost lost her supper.

Getting out the first time had been nearly impossible. This time, Gerald would ensure his prisoners remained in his control for as long as he wished.

Josef propelled her through the building. She avoided looking at the exotic animal collection. A cacophony of shouts reached her. He thrust her inside the medical ward, where chaos reigned.

Lincoln stood at the deep sink scrubbing his hands and barking orders. Sasha and Sergei scrambled left and right, clearly unfamiliar with the ward's layout and contents. A patient was lying on a bed to her right leaking blood from multiple GSWs.

Her gaze locked with the man she'd considered a friend. Any shame he might've felt remained locked away as he was in life-saving mode.

"I need you, Audrey."

Betrayal sat on her tongue like bile. "How could you...?"

A man stepped from the shadowed alcove on her left.

Gerald. His face was grey, but his gunmetal eyes were as ruthless as she remembered.

"If you don't do everything in your power to save my son, Miss Harris, your marine will die sooner rather than later. It won't be a pleasant death, of that you can be sure."

His son? Shock held her immobile.

Finally, she found her voice. "You want me to help your son? Release Julian."

Gerald's eyes narrowed to slits. "No one makes demands of the Jungle King."

Her insides quelled. "My assistance for his freedom. It's a fair trade."

"Fair isn't in my dictionary." Gesturing to the twins, he barked, "Ready one of the torture rooms for Sergeant Tan."

"No!" The last of her defiance drained away. "Leave him alone. I-I'll help."

Lincoln pulled on gloves and instructed her where to find IV fluids. Audrey didn't have a choice. Springing into action, she made quick work of sterilizing her hands and inserting the port into his hand.

"What's his name?" she asked, trying hard to focus on the patient instead of the danger surrounding her. "Age? Medications?"

"Zachary. Twenty-six. No meds. No known drug allergies." Lincoln cut away his tattered shirt. "Help me turn him."

She reached across the bed to assist. "Exit wound?"

Lincoln nodded. "Yes. Bullet cleared the body. We'll need to check for internal damage."

"What's that sucking noise?" Gerald had stationed himself at the foot of the bed.

"Pneumothorax. Collapsed lung," she clarified. "We'll fix it."

She cleansed the chest area. Using the clear dressing Lincoln gave her, she quickly taped it over Zachary's wound, leaving a small opening for air to escape. While Lincoln retrieved a portable ultrasound device, she cranked the bed to raise his upper body to the desired angle.

"Where can I find lidocaine jelly?" she said.

He pointed to the cabinets behind the bed. "Chest tube and drainage system are in there."

"What about his leg?" Gerald said.

"We'll deal with that next," Lincoln replied, passing the ultrasound wand over Zachary's abdomen and studying the screen. "Whoever applied the tourniquet did a smart thing."

Audrey returned and applied the jelly. Then she took the wand from Lincoln in order to guide his procedure. He made an incision between the patient's ribs and inserted the tube into the chest cavity. Once it was stitched into place, they locked gazes. He gave her a small nod of encouragement.

They weren't out of the woods yet, though. Audrey applied the heart-monitor leads. His heart rate was up, his blood pressure low from blood loss.

"I need to type and cross match him before we address his leg."

"He's O positive. You'll find blood stores in the cooling system."

Audrey dashed to the glass-fronted fridge and masked her surprise at its contents. Antivenom. Blood stores rivaling any top-notch hospital. A variety of medications. Black-market medicine at its finest.

At Zachary's bedside, Lincoln uttered some choice words. Gerald immediately stiffened.

"What is it?"

"Nothing to worry about. The bullet's lodged in his

thigh, that's all. Audrey and I will have to remove it and repair the damage to his artery."

"Do you have everything you require for the procedure?" Gerald demanded.

Audrey looked at Lincoln. They didn't have support staff or lab technicians. There wasn't an anesthesiologist. The list continued.

Avoiding her gaze, he exuded a confidence she didn't feel. "I do."

"Good." Gerald studied Zachary's face. "Get on with it, then."

"You and your henchmen have to wait outside," she told him.

"I don't believe you're in the position to give orders."

"This is supposed to be a sterile environment," she growled. "It's your son's life. If you don't mind taking unnecessary risks, then neither do I."

He shot her a black scowl before ushering the twins from the room. He took up residence on the other side of the observation window.

Lincoln had already donned a cap and mask. He handed her the same and returned Zachary's bed to the regular position.

"This is madness, Lincoln. Renegade medicine."

"It's a simple repair job."

"Where's the electrocautery machine? Pulse oximeter? What happens if we get in there, and there's bone or tissue damage?"

His gaze punched hers. "We'll react accordingly."

"Lincoln—"

"There's no sense arguing, Audrey. You can rail at me afterward."

She tamped down her objections and forced her mind from the fury simmering in her veins. The patient—no

matter who he was or what he'd done—deserved her full
concentration. The surgery was relatively straightforward.
Zachary was fortunate the bullet hadn't inflicted serious
damage. He remained stable throughout the procedure,
a small blessing in the midst of uncertainty.

The tightness bracketing Lincoln's mouth finally eased.

"Let's close him up."

Gerald, who'd been hovering outside like an ominous
cloud, reentered the ward, his henchmen behind him. He
gazed upon his son's face for long moments.

"Sergei. Sasha. You will join me in my private quarters."

Audrey removed her mask and gloves and discarded
them, unnerved by the twins' nearness. Their very presence confirmed Officer Dunn was guilty, like Craddock.

If they were gleeful she'd been recaptured, they didn't
show it. Like robots, they nodded and opened the door.

Gerald clasped Lincoln's upper arm. "Thank you,
cousin."

Audrey couldn't have heard that right. Gerald hailed
from Eastern Europe. Judging by their appearance, they
did share hair color and skin tone. They both had promi-
nent noses. That's where the similarities ended.

"He's not out of the woods, yet," he warned.

"You won't leave him alone."

Lincoln shook his head. "Wouldn't dream of it."

Gerald's focus came to rest on her. Her mouth dried.
The adrenaline rush that had carried her through Zachary's
life-saving procedure was fading, leaving uncertainty and
dread in its wake.

"You will remain with Lincoln until I order otherwise,"
he commanded. "Try another stunt like the last one, and
you will regret it."

He was almost to the door when she called after him.

"Where's Julian?"

Lincoln shot her a warning glance. Gerald's back was rigid as he turned. "He's in a holding cell."

"With one of your creatures?"

"For the moment, he's alone." He looked at his son. "Keep Zachary comfortable and well, and Sergeant Tan will enjoy his last days in peace."

The crime boss didn't give her any time to pose more questions. The door closed with a hard click.

She fisted her hands at her sides. "I want to see him."

Lincoln sighed and ran his fingers through his hair. "That's impossible."

"As impossible as my best friend's fiancé being related to an evil crime lord?"

A grimace marred his features. "Audrey, you don't understand—"

"You're right, I don't." She casually moved to the patient's bedside. "I can't think of an explanation or excuse that would make sense of this." Her hand hovered above the tube inserted into Zachary's chest. "Either you get me to him, or I rip this out and the Jungle Prince suffers potentially fatal complications."

SEVENTEEN

Julian paced the perimeter of the ten-by-ten room, searching for weak points in the cement-block wall or the thick glass insert on the interior wall. He wasn't prepared when the door burst open and Audrey hurled herself into his arms.

His muscles sore from the Taser shock, he staggered back a couple of steps. As her warmth and scent enveloped him, he buried his face in her hair and held her tight.

"You have fifteen minutes."

Julian lifted his head in time to see Lincoln exiting and closing the door. Fury intermingled with the relief of seeing Audrey.

Her entire body trembled. Easing away, he caressed her cheek and peered deep into her eyes. "Tell me."

"I was forced to dig a bullet out of Gerald's son." She licked her lips. "Lincoln and I managed to stabilize him, but he's lost a lot of blood, and there's the risk of infection and complications from the procedure."

"His son, huh?" Julian released her in an effort to organize his thoughts. "If something goes sideways, you'll be held accountable."

"Julian, our future is sealed." Despondency dripped from her words. "Whether Zachary lives or dies doesn't change anything for us."

He rubbed his hands up and down her arms. "Don't do that. Don't give up. You fight until the very last second, understand?"

Her chin wobbled. "Why has God allowed this? I've never professed to be perfect. I mess up all the time. I *have* endeavored to honor Him with my words and actions, to give Him first place in my heart."

He sent a silent prayer upward. "I can't answer that. But I'm reminded of my mom's favorite Old Testament account. Remember Joseph? Sold into slavery, falsely accused and imprisoned?"

Her lashes swept down. "God caused his guards to show him favor. He brought him into a position of power, gifted him with a family and enabled him to save thousands of lives."

"Including his brothers, who'd sold him off because of jealousy. I remember the verse to this day. 'But as for you, you meant evil against me—but God meant it for good, in order to bring it about as it is this day, to save many people alive.'"

A tear slid down her cheek, and it arrowed straight through his heart. If only he had it in his power to shield her from this trial.

Gently brushing away the tear, he pulled her close and began to pray aloud. It wasn't a polished prayer. It was rusty and messy and disjointed, but reaching out to his Lord was a soothing, healing balm.

He stroked her disheveled braid. "This isn't a surprise to Him, you know. He's still in control."

She dashed the wetness from her cheeks and tugged on his short sleeve. "Let me see your back. Did they remove the barbs?"

"I'm fine."

"Let me see."

Julian sighed and waited for her reaction. She lifted his T-shirt and gasped.

Turning to face her, he shrugged. "They weren't as gentle as an ER nurse would've been, but I've endured worse."

"You'll need antibiotic cream, at the very least. How's your arm?"

"Also fine, believe it or not." He flexed his fingers and rotated his wrist. "I've done my best to baby it."

"How long before Brady or Cade discovers we're missing?"

"It's after midnight, so they're both snoozing. Brady promised to bring groceries during his lunch break."

"A lot can happen in twelve hours."

Plus, he might assume they were out conducting their amateur investigation. Even if Brady surmised they were in trouble, he had few options. Julian had disclosed the warehouse's location to his friend, but he'd also warned him there were dirty cops in the local department. Not to mention he'd be implicating himself if he approached law enforcement with his information.

"That's right," he told her, masking his concern. "Like finding a way out of here."

"I don't know…"

"I do." He clasped her hand. "We managed it once before. We'll think of something."

Lincoln returned then.

Audrey inhaled sharply. "I'm not ready."

The surgeon had the grace to look pained. "I'll bring you back later. Right now, Gerald can't know you've left the ward."

"I don't care about Gerald."

Julian squeezed her hand. "It's okay."

It wasn't, but he had to reassure her. Had to project calm and confidence, for her sake.

"No one will harm him," she stated, glaring at Lincoln. "Give me your word."

His gaze met Julian's. "As long as you remain Zachary's compliant caretaker, you both should be safe."

Her hands balled. "You said *should.*"

Lincoln tapped his shoe. "There's no more time."

Julian gave her a gentle push. "Go."

Her torment plain, she went with Lincoln. Julian sank onto the hard cement ground and began to pray. The helicopter accident had ended in tragedy. He couldn't begin to second-guess God's purpose. Nor would he try. This was where trust and faith came into play.

"Lie down and get some rest, Audrey."

Lincoln nodded to the empty beds before adjusting Zachary's blanket.

"I can't sleep." While her body cried out for rest, her anxious mind would never let her succumb to that vulnerable state.

A heavy sigh gusted out of him. "Pulling you into this was the last thing we wanted."

She zeroed in on the word *we.* "You and Chasity."

"Please sit down before you pass out," he said, gesturing to the bed farthest from Zach's. When she'd perched on the mattress, he dragged over the single chair in the room, straddled it and looped his arms over the top. "I didn't plan on enlisting her aid. It happened by accident. We were having a nice dinner. There was an emergency. Sergei and Sasha showed up to escort me..." He threaded his fingers through his hair. "I was relieved, to be honest, to have this part of my life exposed to her."

Could he not see his utter selfishness? "You didn't worry what would happen if, like me, she refused to join the organization?"

His eyes darkened. "Chasity was drowning in debt. She saw an opportunity to climb out."

"She's obviously not struggling anymore." Audrey reviewed the last few months from a different perspective.

Her friend had started shopping at high-end boutiques. Enjoyed expensive spa treatments and weekend getaways. "I assumed the perks were courtesy of her new boyfriend. You know, because you have such a generous heart."

"This doesn't have to be a morality issue. We're helping patients, plain and simple."

"Criminals, Lincoln. You treat gang members. You're a puppet for a crime boss. Think about the patients you endangered at Onslow General for that man."

"We take every precaution to ensure no harm is done."

Audrey scrubbed her hands down her face. How could she have misjudged her friends?

"Isn't your salary enough to sustain your lifestyle?"

"You have no idea how expensive divorce can be. Gina's lawyer ensured she would continue to live in luxury. The kids' private school alone costs me thousands each year."

"Yet you live in a sprawling mansion alone and drive a flashy car. Don't make it sound like you had no other options."

"I have a reputation to uphold. Besides, Chasity deserves the best."

"Where is Chasity? Why isn't she here?"

"She's on shift."

"Fortunate for me, right? I got to take over her job."

"Part of your current troubles rests on your shoulders," he said with a touch of imperiousness. "We both tried to dissuade you from sticking your nose where it didn't belong. You're as stubborn as they come."

She shot off the bed. "Don't you dare blame me!"

Gerald swept into the ward like an avenging war general. "What is the meaning of this outburst?"

Lincoln jumped to his feet and moved to shield her from his cousin's wrath. "She has questions, Gerald. It's only natural."

"Get her out of here," he snapped. "I won't have her hindering Zachary's recuperation."

"I'm sure she's calm now. Aren't you, Audrey?"

Gerald crooked his finger, and the twins advanced. "Put her in with Sergeant Tan. She can return in an hour or two, if she promises to be on her best behavior."

She instinctively backed away. The last time they'd come after her, she'd wound up in the sea.

Again, Lincoln moved in front of her. "I'll take her. Stay with Zach for a few minutes."

Gerald reluctantly acquiesced.

Lincoln marched her through the warehouse to the holding cell. Before punching in the door code, he said, "I'll do my best to protect you, but you have to avoid riling him."

"He already tried to kill us. You're aware of that?"

The skin around his eye twitched. "The fact that he is family allows me some influence. I will try and convince him to release you."

"Your confidence is reassuring," she retorted, hurt and confused.

"He's used to calling the shots. Gerald has cultivated an empire, and he goes to great lengths to protect his interests. I wish you had let this go."

"Julian and I are in danger because of your choices, Lincoln." She poked his chest. "You have to make this right."

The grim turn of his mouth, combined with the dull light in his eyes, deflated what was left of her hope.

He punched in the code and opened the door. "I'll come and get you later."

Julian rose from his position on the floor. "What's happened?"

"I don't think we can count on Lincoln to intervene," she told him. "I have this terrible feeling he's going to let Gerald do whatever he wants to us."

"You can't know that for sure."

"I did manage to see the code he used to unlock the door."

His eyes widened. "You did?"

"I have to sneak away from the ward somehow and free you."

"We're familiar with the layout. That will work to our advantage." Frowning, he scraped his hand over his jaw. "I don't like to think what would happen if you're discovered. I'd be trapped in here. Unable to help."

His unease at that prospect permeated the air. Such a scenario was their worst nightmare.

Audrey didn't want to wait for Chasity's arrival. Lincoln's failure to pledge his assistance was a major blow. He wasn't as dear to her, however. Chas was the sister she'd never had. Her betrayal felt like a death. She couldn't look into her face and see the same resignation, the same unwillingness to help, that Lincoln displayed.

"Then I'll have to make sure I'm not discovered."

Julian's protests invaded her restless sleep. Her first thought was that he was being dragged out of their prison. She jerked off the cold, slick floor, the folded sweatshirt serving as her pillow forgotten as she rushed to his side.

"Julian, wake up."

The instant she grazed his hand, he was alert and upright.

"I didn't mean to startle you," she said. "You were having a nightmare."

"I'm glad you woke me. I hadn't intended to fall asleep." He rolled his neck to get the kinks out. "Did you get any rest?"

"Some." The only window in the room was blacked-out from this side, making it impossible to gauge how much time had passed. "You kept repeating a name," she said softly. "Ross. Short for Rossello, I presume?"

"Yeah." Pulling his knees to his chest, he took his time retying his shoelace. He looked tired and vulnerable.

Audrey quelled the urge to smooth his rumpled hair. Instead, she busied her hands untangling her braid.

She'd gone to the four funerals to support her father, as well as the family members. While Anthony Rossello had been a single man, he had scores of siblings, cousins and aunts and uncles. The church had been filled to bursting with people wishing to pay their respects. Julian had been in attendance, of course, but their paths hadn't crossed.

"Were you closer to Rossello than the others?"

"Actually, he and I butted heads a lot. We didn't think alike, and we both attempted to assert our will over the other."

"I see."

Propping one arm atop his bent knee, he rested against the cement-block wall. "I've had nightmares off and on since it happened. He's the one I'm always trying to save."

"Maybe it's your subconscious mind hashing out the issues between you."

His gaze became vague, unfocused, and she knew he was replaying those terrible events.

"Ross clung to life the longest," he uttered, his voice like gravel. "He gave me messages to pass on to his parents and siblings. I argued with him. Yelled at him, demanding he hang on. Nothing worked. Nothing I tried worked. Maybe if I'd had more medical knowledge, I could've kept him alive a few minutes longer until the ambulance arrived."

His sorrow held her in its grip. She brought his hand to her cheek. "I'm sorry, my love. So very sorry."

He looked at her then. Really looked at her. There were no walls, no defensive shields. Audrey felt as if she'd been gifted a rare glimpse into his soul. The entirety of his pent-up pain, guilt and grief enveloped her. When she'd thought that she couldn't bear the brunt of it a second longer, the coppery gold depths shimmered and cleared, made beautiful with wonder and gratitude, appreciation and fondness.

Flipping his hand over so that his palm cradled her face, he said, "If there's a silver lining in this dark cloud, Audrey Harris, it's knowing you."

Her heart kicked and bucked. The way he was looking at her made her feel like she could soar right up to the sky.

The tender moment was shattered in the next instant. Sergei bumbled into the room.

"Emergency with Mr. Zachary. Come."

She instinctively recoiled from his meaty hand. His upper lip curled. "I will carry you if you resist."

Julian unfurled like a jungle cat and sprang to his feet. "Let Lincoln handle it. Or call his fiancée."

Sergei's fists bunched. He took a menacing step toward Julian.

"I'll go." Audrey clutched Julian's shoulder. "It's okay. I'll be back as soon as I can."

His eyes spit fire. "When she's done your bidding," he growled, "see that you give her something to eat and drink."

Sergei's scowl deepened as he held the door for her. She glanced back over her shoulder, soaking in his precious face. Every time she left him, she worried it would be the last time she saw him alive.

EIGHTEEN

She'd called him *my love*.

The endearment had spilled from her lips in earnest, yet he didn't think it had even registered in her mind. It led him to believe she said it often and with casual intent, like when a restaurant server called him *honey* or *sweetie*.

He completed another set of sit-ups. Sweat poured off of him. He glanced at the bottle of water and sandwich Sergei had left. His mouth was sandpaper-dry, and he needed to replace the fluids he was losing. He resisted the temptation. Gerald was demented. Lacing Julian's food or drink with drugs wasn't out of the realm of possibility.

My love.

Would she be embarrassed if she knew her eyes had taken on the brilliance of sapphires when she'd said it?

Ignoring the twinges in his back where the Taser barbs had burrowed into his skin, he counted out twenty more sit-ups.

She'd been gone a long time this time. Four hours, give or take.

He hated not being able to see her, hated not knowing if she was tending to Gerald's son or being dragged onto that boat again.

They were going to have to decide on a plan soon. He had no doubt he was being kept alive as leverage, and as soon as Zachary's condition became less precarious—or Chasity finally made an appearance—he'd become disposable. And so would Audrey.

The door opened. He jumped up, expecting her. But it was Sergei.

"Where's Audrey?"

Sergei noted the uneaten sandwich and cocked an eyebrow. "Let's go."

Julian debated his options. He had nothing on him besides the plastic wrap he'd removed from the bread and turkey and slid into his pocket. Not a hazardous weapon, but stuffed inside someone's mouth? A momentary distraction.

He studied Sergei. The big man looked cool as a cucumber. No telltale sweating. No fist flexing or bulging veins. He didn't appear to be here to carry out a kill order.

"I said, let's go." He waved his hand, the Taser gun in his grip.

Julian winced. He'd been Tasered once during training. It had been on purpose, of course, and far less traumatic than this most recent incident.

He wasn't keen on repeating the experience. On edge, he passed the goon and preceded him into the open space. An elderly man was washing the outside of the piranha tank. His gaze briefly touched Julian's before darting away. The living area set up to their right was empty.

Sergei prodded him to go that way, the opposite direction of the medical ward.

"How's Zachary?" he asked, dragging his feet.

No answer.

"The emergency you mentioned earlier. Has that been addressed?"

"Stop here."

He obeyed, his neck and shoulder muscles bunching.

Sergei opened a door and flicked on the light.

"You brought me to the bathroom?"

"Go in or not. I'm following orders."

Julian was secretly glad of the chance. Closing the door, he drank from the faucet and splashed cold water over his hair and face. He swiped several paper towels and, folding them into thin squares, tucked them into his back pocket.

He emerged from the bathroom, and his keeper ordered him to return to the holding cell. He dreaded returning to the bare, drab gray box of a room.

Julian could take out Sergei. The old man at the tanks wasn't going to intervene. Adrenaline bolted through him, flooding him with energy he had trouble bridling.

Bide your time, Tan.

He could hear Ross muttering the warning through their shared comms.

This ain't the time to be hasty, he'd drawl.

Audrey's safety was paramount. He couldn't mount an attack until he was certain she was leaving *with* him.

They turned the corner. The first thing Julian noticed was that Audrey was alone. The second thing was that she was punching in the door code.

She'd slipped out of the ward, like she'd said she would.

Sergei noticed, too. He roared an epithet, raised his Taser gun and started for her.

Julian sprinted and tackled Sergei, knocking him down just before he reached Audrey. They hit the floor hard. The Taser clattered out of reach.

In the top position, he landed a blow to the man's head. It didn't faze him. Sergei got his hands around his throat and cut off his air supply.

Julian maneuvered his knee against his windpipe and applied pressure. His eyes bugged. Letting go, Sergei bucked him off and clambered to his feet.

Audrey seized Julian's arm. "Here. Take this."

She put something hard and thin into his hand. A scalpel, bless her.

Sergei did not appreciate her resourcefulness. His skin turning a mottled pink, he came at them like a raging bull.

Julian used the man's rage to his advantage, easily dodging him and spinning to the side. Then he sank the scalpel into the soft flesh between his shoulder and neck. The big man fumbled. It was the opening they needed.

Grabbing her hand, he urged her into a sprint. Past the tanks. Past the mock living room.

Behind them, Sergei's calls for help were answered. Footsteps raced after them.

They were almost to the double doors he knew led to the control room and main entrance when they surged open and in walked Chasity.

NINETEEN

Chasity—her college roommate, her coworker, her friend—stood between them and freedom. Between certain death and a chance at survival.

Audrey's surroundings blurred. Chasity's blue eyes were rife with indecision in her ash-hued face. Anguish pinched her mouth. She had a choice to make. Side with her criminal fiancé and his corrupt cousin or choose to do the right thing.

Audrey couldn't speak, but she was certain her plea was stamped on her features.

A shot rang out. Julian's arm came around her, shielding her.

The ping was followed by shattering glass and whooshing water. She couldn't resist a peek behind her. Silvery piranhas gushed to the floor in a flapping, gape-mouthed river.

Josef was racing after them, full steam ahead.

Chasity called her name. "This way!"

Audrey's feet moved before her brain had time to process the sacrifice her friend was making. Gratitude flooded her as Chas led the way to the main entrance.

"There's a guard on the other side," she said over her shoulder. "Be prepared."

Julian released Audrey's hand. "Roger that."

"We can take my car," she said. "I have a remote control for the gate."

"Don't wait on me," he warned.

"We aren't leaving you," Audrey said.

"You're stubborn, you know that?" he huffed.

The next second, they were out in the bright sunshine. Audrey was momentarily disoriented.

"Hurry!" Chas grabbed her hand and tugged.

The shiny new sedan was angled close to the warehouse. Chas tossed her the keys.

"Get behind the wheel."

Audrey didn't like the determined gleam in her friend's eyes. "You're coming with us."

Beneath the warehouse's overhang, she saw the goon sprawled unconscious on the ground and Julian racing to join them, an automatic rifle slung over his shoulder.

The main doors banged open. Josef emerged with Sasha on his heels.

"I have to stay with Lincoln," Chas said.

"They'll kill you!"

"No, I don't think so. I'm too valuable. Nurses have more access to drugs than doctors, right?" A wobbly smile flashed.

"Right."

Julian reached them. "No time to waste, ladies. We go now or not at all."

Audrey had a terrible feeling that her friend had underestimated Gerald, but she couldn't force her to leave.

Resignation twisting her features, Chasity stepped back.

As soon as Audrey got in, Julian followed suit. She whipped the car in Reverse, nearly giving them whiplash, then gunned the gas. The car lurched forward. Julian hit the gate remote, then twisted in the seat, the huge gun atop his lap.

"What's happening?" Audrey demanded.

"Josef's got Chasity. He's shoving her into an SUV.

Probably thinks she can lead him to hideouts we may use if they lose sight of us."

Fear for her friend's safety clashed with her own survival instincts. Barreling through the opening and onto the street, she gripped the wheel so hard her hands ached.

"I should've let you drive."

"You'll do fine. I'll be the navigator."

"Where are we going?"

He was silent a moment. "Storefront, but not until we lose Josef. Stick to the side roads."

They might be out of the warehouse, but they couldn't afford to be caught by military police or civilian law enforcement.

He guided her through the waterfront's choppy grid of side streets. It being a Monday afternoon, there were plenty of employees in this business district who might call and report a high-speed chase. But she couldn't focus on that now. Josef's green SUV was gaining on them.

"Turn right."

She yanked the wheel. The tires squealed as they careened onto a two-lane highway.

Behind her, a car horn blasted. She hadn't thought to look for oncoming traffic.

Perspiration dampened her neck, and her chest felt heavy. Julian's hand settled on her knee.

"You're doing good. Hang in there."

In her side mirror, she saw the SUV enter the oncoming lane and attempt to blast past the sports car behind her. That driver, already disgruntled because she'd cut him off, increased his speed.

"He's not going to let them pass," she cried out.

Audrey returned her gaze to the road ahead. A heavily loaded dump truck was approaching. He blasted his horn to warn Josef.

Julian gave her knee a light squeeze. "Speed up."

Her body taut, she glanced out her window. "Julian, they're going to crash if Josef doesn't do something."

"Maintain your current speed. We need to be out of the field of debris."

She heeded his warning. Focused entirely on the road ahead. Spindly pine trees flashed past them. In the distance, water shimmered in the winter sun. The road rose up ahead to meet a high-arching bridge. Josef couldn't be allowed to catch up on that bridge. A hard nudge perfectly landed could send their small sedan careening off the edge.

A single, slow hiss left Julian's lips. Audrey's gaze flicked to the rearview mirror. The scene was like an orchestrated movie stunt. The dump truck's brake lights flaring red. The sports car keeping pace with the SUV. Josef's last-minute decision to jerk right.

Too late.

The SUV's right wheel glanced off the sports car's bumper, sending the vehicle straight into the dump truck's front end.

Head-on collision.

"Don't slow down," he commanded, gripping her shoulder. "Keep driving."

Tears choked her. "Chasity."

"You can't help her." He muttered something under his breath. "Cars are stopping. Someone will call nine-one-one."

The car flew up and over the bridge. On the other side, he instructed her to pull over, where they changed places. They drove for what seemed like an eternity, neither speaking. The silence was like a funeral pause.

Audrey kept replaying the accident. The SUV had

rolled and flipped multiple times before rocking to a stop—a mangled heap of steaming metal.

By the time Julian jimmied the storefront's locked door, the tears were flowing down her cheeks. He shepherded her inside and, after closing and securing the door, hugged her close.

"Go ahead, sweetheart. Let it out."

Overwhelming devastation sucked her into a whirlpool of grief, and she couldn't stem the sorrow. Julian offered comfort and reassurance. He was her refuge. Her friend. He was the man she trusted with her life…and with her heart.

His soothing words and tender ministrations calmed her.

"I've soaked your shirt," she said, slipping out of his arms and swiping at her wet cheeks.

"I don't mind." He handed her neatly folded paper towels. "Come upstairs and drink something."

She trudged up the stairs behind him.

"Have you had anything to eat today?" he said.

"I told Lincoln I wasn't hungry."

At the thought of Lincoln's reaction to the news of Chasity's almost certain demise, her eyes welled up again. Her stomach churned. She deliberately tamped down the fresh wave of emotion.

"What was the emergency? The one Sergei insisted you help with?"

"Zachary had become agitated and ripped out his chest tube."

"Ouch."

"It was chaotic for a while. He was having trouble breathing, which led to him panicking. Gerald shouting orders at us didn't help."

"But you got him stabilized?"

"I'm confident he'll recover with no lasting problems."

In the kitchen, Julian removed a fruit juice container and poured a good amount into an old-fashioned blue glass. "Drink this."

"Zachary will keep Gerald preoccupied, but for how long?"

He poured some for himself, as well. When he'd downed the contents, he set it in the sink and turned to look at her.

She took another sip. "I don't know what you're thinking, but I have a feeling I won't like it."

"I'm considering turning myself in."

"You're not serious."

"Hear me out. We've got three groups after us. We can't hole up here forever. Eventually, someone will recognize us or report suspicious activity. I'm sure Cade and Tori would agree to hide you somewhere. Meanwhile, I'll return to base and let the provost marshal investigate. With me in custody, the heat on you will lessen."

"I'm not on board with that plan. Think of another one."

"It's the best one I've got." He tunneled his fingers through his hair and sighed. "The marine corps is our best chance at a fair hearing. I can feed them information and assist in the investigation with a clear head if I know you're safe."

"You won't be safe."

He stepped over and cupped her elbows, holding her close. "I will be among my own. I can't say the same of a civilian jail system."

Exhaustion, combined with her current mental state, made significant decisions impossible. "We should wait until tomorrow to discuss it further."

He didn't agree, that much as obvious. But he gave in to her wishes.

Releasing her, he gestured to the windows overlooking the woods and church beyond. "Just in case Gerald installed a tracker on Chasity's car, I'm going to park it a couple of streets away and hike back."

She didn't like the idea of him walking around town on a busy weekday. Sounds of activity leaked through the windows. Cars passing by. Pedestrians chatting. Delivery trucks dropping packages at nearby shops.

He tipped up her chin. "Don't worry. I'll keep my head down."

Brady ended up spending the night at the storefront. He wasn't able to make it on his lunch break, as promised, so he came straight from the air station Monday evening, paper sacks stuffed with juicy cheeseburgers and fries. He'd even thought to include chocolate shakes piled with clouds of whipped cream. Fast food had never tasted so good. After Julian and Audrey devoured their meals, they told him about their harrowing ordeal.

The pilot was as stoic as they came, but even he couldn't mask his shock and dismay. He brushed aside their warnings and insisted on staying. Before leaving for work Tuesday morning, he promised to return at lunchtime with more food and necessities. Julian could only hope for a chance to repay his friends for what they'd done.

Midmorning, they decided to pass the time with a card game they'd unearthed in the supply closet. The downstairs door opened without warning. Voices ricocheted off the bare walls.

Audrey bolted to her feet, fright draining the color from her cheeks.

Julian put his finger to his lips. Whoever was down

there, they weren't looking for fugitives. The feminine voices were cheerful and friendly. The one male inserted a word or two.

He scooped up the cards and pointed to the bathroom. Nodding, she rushed into the tiny space first. Julian followed. Audrey had to inch between the toilet and the shower to give him room.

"Who are they?" she whispered.

Kicking up his shoulder, he didn't completely close the door. The trio seemed to be drifting closer to the main entrance. If they came upstairs, they'd see their belongings and possibly report suspected squatting. *Please, Lord Jesus, let us catch a break.*

"The building's been vacant for several months, but as you can see, the owners keep it maintained. They pay to keep the electricity and water hooked up."

Julian closed and locked the door. Turning around, he rested his weight against it. "Must be a real estate agent showing the place to potential renters," he whispered.

She finger-combed her red waves with short, jerky strokes. After supper last evening, they'd both taken advantage of the chance to wash up. Audrey had emerged wearing a pink sweatshirt emblazoned with the words *Marine Wife*. She'd blushed beneath the weight of his stare. Brady had shrugged and blamed the fact he wasn't accustomed to shopping for anything, much less women's clothing.

More and more, in those rare, quiet moments he wasn't being chased or shot at, Julian's mind entertained thoughts of a future with her. It was beyond tempting. He used to be afraid of further disappointing his father. Now, he was more afraid of disappointing Audrey, of failing her. Hurting her.

Their heavy, slow treads marked their decision to in-

ventory the upper floor. Of course, they would want to
see it.

Audrey pressed her lips together in a tight line. Aban-
doning her hair-combing, she fit her palms together in a
prayer gesture and squeezed her eyes shut.

Julian kept his gaze trained on her.

Would they be discovered? Trapped in a bathroom
awaiting the police?

"What's all this?" one of the women asked.

"I have no idea." That must be the real estate agent. "It
appears someone has been using the kitchen."

"Are those sleeping bags?"

The agent made a tsking noise. "The owners will have
to be notified."

"I'd contact the police." The man's voice boomed.

Audrey's lids popped open. Her pained gaze met his,
and he wanted to soothe away her hurt and worry. He
wanted—no, *needed*—to see her happy and carefree
again. How many times had he ridden in the elevator
with her? Nodding instead of speaking. Noticing her sweet
smile, her perky ponytail and cherry slushies. Now he
wished he'd engaged her in conversation. Invited her to
his favorite Chinese restaurant.

Lost opportunities loomed large.

"This is a safe neighborhood. I'm sure there's a good
explanation." The agent was attempting to reassure her
clients. "Let me show you the bathroom."

Audrey's lips parted. Julian's blood turned to sludge.
He maintained even pressure against the aged wood.

The knob turned. Jiggled.

"It won't budge."

"Do you have a tool to unlock it?" The man spoke
again.

"Not with me."

"We can see it next time," the other woman chimed in. "I'd like to go now in case the squatter returns."

They retreated downstairs. The back door opened and closed.

"Julian, what now?"

Without phones, they couldn't reach out to Brady. "We wait until they leave, then start walking. Too risky to use Chasity's car. There's a public park three blocks from here, where we can make plans to meet up with Cade or Brady."

They crept out of the bathroom and, going to the windows, spied on the trio. The couple climbed into their vehicle and left. The agent paced along the buildings, her phone glued to her ear. She did not look pleased.

"Who's she talking to?" Audrey wondered aloud.

"Probably her realty company." She ended that call, then made a second, brief one.

"She's not leaving."

Julian had a bad feeling, and for good reason—a Jacksonville PD patrol car rambled down the lane. A man exited the car, his steely gaze roving over the building's rear facade.

Audrey wrapped her fingers around his. "This is the end, isn't it?"

TWENTY

She was going to be separated from Julian. She'd be interrogated. Locked in a jail cell. He'd be whisked off to Camp Lejeune and the provost marshal.

Would he ever be released?

Would she?

"Hide in the shower," he ordered. "I'll surrender. He won't have cause to search."

"No."

His eyes pleaded with her. "There's no reason for you to get caught up in this. Brady will take you somewhere where Gerald and crooked cops like Craddock can't reach you."

"I can't let you face them alone. You'll need me to corroborate the facts."

A car door slammed outside, followed by loud voices. They looked at each other.

"That sounds like Brady."

Resuming their positions at the window, Audrey felt as if she might crumple to the floor and not get up for years. Brady was indeed down there. His flight suit gave him authority and presence as he spoke rapidly to the officer and agent.

"He's good," she murmured. "No outward sign of nerves."

"Takes nerves of steel to do what he does miles above the earth."

"He's also got incredible timing."

A thorough explanation later, he'd satisfied the others'

concern and waved them on their way. Julian and Audrey met him at the top of the stairs.

Folding his aviator sunglasses and sliding them into his breast pocket, he planted his hands on his hips and regarded them both with relief.

"You're fortunate I skipped breakfast and decided to take an early lunch."

Julian gave him a hearty hug. "*Mahalo*, brother."

"No need to thank me." Striding to the kitchen, he peered through the blinds. "I've got fresh sub sandwiches in the car. Let's give it another five or ten minutes, and I'll go get them."

"What did you say to them?" Julian asked.

"I produced my military ID and my door key. Explained that I sometimes stop here for lunch instead of driving home." Sunlight glinted on his shorn blond locks. "Makes sense. I only have an hour break."

"What about the sleeping bags? They didn't mention them?" Julian asked.

Letting the blinds flick into place, he shrugged. "I told them I let a friend crash here for a few days while he searched for more permanent housing. I didn't know Uncle Randall had hired a real estate agent. Next time it happens, you can hide out in the attic."

Julian shook his head. "That was too close. I have to go to PMO."

"The military police?" Brady's eyebrows met his hairline. "You sure that's wise?"

"We can't run forever."

His gaze locked with hers. Audrey's heart sank. She'd gotten to know him, could read his moods and guess the gist of his thoughts. Julian had decided to sacrifice his freedom in a bid to spare her. He wouldn't be dissuaded by arguments or tears or threats. She feared that, if she refused to cooperate, he'd reach an agreement with Brady behind her back and disappear in the middle of the night. In his view, that would be the noble choice.

"Before you turn yourself in, let's go to my dad."

His forehead creased. "We agreed he's better off left out of it."

"He knows you, Julian. He trusts you. How do you think your reception will be if you drive through the main base gate alone?"

Brady snorted. "Choice words. Weapons drawn. Tan on the ground eating concrete."

She suppressed a shudder. "Exactly. Now consider this—Gunnery Sergeant Trent Harris making a few phone calls and arranging for PMO to come to us."

"No drama. Private, personal escort." Brady nodded. "I like it. What do you say, Tan?"

Thrusting both hands through his hair, he paced the length of the room. "I'd rather not involve you at all, Audrey. If they see you, they'll report it."

"I can remain out of sight." Or she could go with him, she thought.

The air in the room thinned as Julian considered her suggestion. Brady leaned against the kitchen counter, arms folded over his chest and legs crossed at the ankle, alternatively watching her and then his friend.

"Let's do it."

Amid the dread of the unknown, Audrey experienced a glimmer of hope. Maybe, just maybe, they'd survive this ordeal and be stronger for it.

Brady arranged the meeting. He chose a lesser-used section of a public park located smack in the heart of Jacksonville. The sun hovered above the treetops in the bleary sky. It was a brisk winter evening, which meant only the hardiest of outdoor enthusiasts would brave the cold.

"How did he sound?" Audrey asked again, one big bundle of nerves.

"Like a worried father," Brady patiently replied. "He's anxious to see you."

Julian's gaze did a thorough inspection of the parking lot, restrooms and picnic tables. Scrubby pines and spindle-limbed trees formed a natural border on their right, extending far into the distance. Another thick copse on their left hampered their view of the rest of the park. Layers of dead leaves and pine needles formed a carpet on either side of a wide stream. Beyond the tables, playground equipment on a bed of mulch stood silent, and farther still was a covered pavilion. The stark serenity of the scene was in direct opposition to the turmoil inside her.

She looked at Julian again. He hadn't spoken a single word since they'd left the storefront. To the casual observer, he appeared tranquil and in control. She'd spent enough time with him to see past the mask. His neck was stiff, his jaw like granite and his eyes narrowed, the skin around them tight.

Why wouldn't he be on edge? He was about to see his superior and answer for his absence, then be taken into custody.

Her stomach rolled. This was a better alternative to Gerald's form of punishment, but that didn't make it any easier to bear.

She wasn't going to emerge unscathed, either. The authorities, civilian or otherwise, would take her in for as long as it took to ascertain her innocence.

Seated beside her in the backseat, Julian eventually noticed her intense scrutiny. His eyebrows lifted slightly. His mouth softened, and his beautiful, tawny eyes warmed to liquid gold. He was looking at her as if she was the only person in the world that mattered.

Audrey's breath caught. He was the most important person in *her* world. His opinions, his hang-ups, his kindness, his sacrificial mind-set—she wanted it all. Julian. The whole man—the tough warrior with the guarded, tender heart.

She loved him, and she would've told him if Brady hadn't been in the car and they weren't about to run the gauntlet.

She didn't know if he loved her back. She hoped. Prayed. Because if he didn't, if he walked out of her life, she wouldn't recover. He'd walk away with her heart.

His gaze dropped to her mouth and, for a charged moment, she thought he might kiss her.

"Gunnery Sergeant Harris is approaching the tables." Brady's announcement shattered the moment.

Audrey twisted toward the door. Through the glass, she recognized her dad's confident stride. Her eyes smarted. He was wearing the blue-and-white ball cap she'd bought him years ago, when they'd left California and relocated in North Carolina.

Julian's hand settled on her shoulder. "Ready?"

"Ready."

She climbed out of the backseat, with Julian close behind. Brady slowly drove away. He'd offered to stick around in case trouble arose, but they'd agreed the risk wasn't worth it. He couldn't be caught helping them.

They started across the grass crisscrossed with sidewalks. A chill breeze swept through the park, tugging wisps of hair from her braid and sneaking beneath her pink sweatshirt. The treetops rustled. Trent hadn't seen them yet. He sat with his back to the parking area, his elbows propped on the wooden table and his head bowed.

She found herself instinctively reaching for Julian, needing the reassurance of his touch. Their fingers threaded together, their palms aligned and she squeezed three times. She intercepted his side glance and smiled.

He didn't know the meaning behind the secret signal. Someday she'd explain. Somewhere along the way, between the murder attempts and evading the authorities, she'd rediscovered her courage. She'd stopped being afraid of love.

When they got within a few yards of the table, she spoke. "Hi, Daddy."

Trent's head popped up. Beneath the cap's brim, his eyes were a tornado of mixed feelings. He stood up and held out his arms.

She was engulfed in his familiar embrace.

"My baby girl."

"I'm sorry for worrying you."

His hold loosened. Peering down at her, he said gruffly, "What's going on, Audrey? The captain was frustratingly closemouthed." His gaze widened. "And what have you done to your hair?"

"Temporary disguise," she said, grimacing. "Brady's been a lifeline. I don't blame him for not offering an explanation." Pulling away, she took hold of Julian's hand. "We've been through an ordeal. Let me warn you—it will sound like something out of a thriller."

Trent's brows snapped together and his eyes spit nails. "I thought we had an understanding, Sergeant. You were supposed to stay away from my daughter. Instead, you embroil her in a public scandal and force her into hiding."

Julian heaved in a breath. She didn't give him a chance to speak. "What do you mean you had an understanding? Dad, please tell me you didn't warn him away like some rigid-minded Victorian aristocrat."

"He's not for you, Audrey."

"I'm not a teenager anymore, and I don't need you orchestrating my life."

"He meant well," Julian said quietly.

"Don't defend him," she retorted. "We can hash this out later. Dad, you have to understand that I'm the one who pulled Julian into the demented world of mob bosses and black-market medicine."

Trent's disbelief plain, he stared hard at them. "The news claims you assaulted a police officer. Is that true?"

"Yes and no."

His nostrils flared. "Start from the beginning, will you?"

"You should sit," she urged.

She noticed his tight-lipped frown when she chose to sit beside Julian. It was important they form a united front. Besides, their time together was growing short. After her dad made his calls, it wouldn't take long for PMO to show up.

As the story poured out, he became less angry and more apprehensive.

Taking off his cap, he rubbed his hand down his face. "This is some predicament you've gotten yourselves into."

Reaching across the table, she rested her hand on his forearm. "I'm sorry."

He patted it. "You've nothing to apologize for. I'm proud of you. You stood up for what was right, even though it was difficult."

In her peripheral vision, she noticed a truck entering the lot and parking near the restrooms. A jogger and his yellow Lab crossed the street and, using the sidewalk, headed toward the other side of the park and the basketball courts.

Giving her dad a challenging stare, she said, "You should apologize to Julian."

Julian shifted on the seat. "That's not necessary."

She turned her head. "You saved my life so many times I've lost count."

"You saved me, too."

Audrey fell into his luminous gaze. The moments they'd shared together—both good and bad—scrolled through her mind. The silence stretched between them until Trent cleared his throat.

"We need to clear your names," he said.

"I pray it's not a lengthy process."

Julian stiffened. "Gunny, we may have a problem."

Trent turned on the bench seat. "Restrooms?"

"Guy in jeans and button-down." Julian rose to his feet.

Audrey thought the man in question resembled Gerald, but he preferred pricey suits and loafers. Besides, he wasn't the kind to carry out orders. He gave them.

"Audrey, get under the table."

Before she could move, wood splintered near her thigh.

"Shooter in the trees!" her dad barked.

Another bullet whizzed through the air, catching Julian off-guard. He went to his knees. Blood soaked through his shirt. Screaming, Audrey scrambled off the bench seat.

"I'm fine. Just grazed," he panted, reaching for her. "Take cover."

He pulled her to the ground beside him. Bullets dug into the earth, spraying bits of dirt and grass in all directions.

Trent returned fire. "I count two. You see any more?"

"Negative." He twisted around. "I don't like this. We're wide open here."

"Retreat to the playground." Trent handed Julian a weapon—he'd come prepared—and jerked his head to indicate the children's equipment. "I'll provide cover, then join you."

Audrey didn't like that plan, but she wasn't going to argue with two seasoned marines. Plus, she needed to get a closer look at Julian's wound. If retreating gave her extra minutes to do that, she'd take them.

Julian seized her hand. "Ready?"

"Ready."

They sprinted across the field. Behind them, Trent got off several more rounds.

Please, God in Heaven, protect my dad.

Pinging against the painted swing set rang in her ears. Bullets meant for them.

Protect us, too, Lord. Lead us to safety.

Julian urged her to speed up. They raced past bouncy animals mounted on metal springs. One of the plastic heads exploded just as she came even with it. A scream ripped from her lips. She flinched and ducked.

"Almost there," Julian yelled, his grip tightening.

He tugged her around yellow stairs that led to a swinging rope bridge. They dove behind a fat, twisting tube slide.

The onslaught continued. How many were out there?

"This way." Julian beckoned her to follow him underneath the structure.

"I imagined I saw Gerald. I guess he really is here."

"If so, he's gotten desperate enough to risk his own hide."

Audrey quickly inspected his arm. "You'll need stitches and antibiotics."

"But it missed bone and major arteries," he stated.

"You're fortunate."

Fired shots, followed by sudden movement at the other opening, startled them. Julian jerked his weapon into position.

"It's me." Trent scanned them from head to toe. "How's the arm?"

Julian removed his finger from the trigger. "Nothing that won't keep."

He looked grim. "I spotted a third man, but there could be more. We can't let them surround us."

Audrey was aware of the silent communication passing between the two. "What now?"

"There's a foot bridge not far from the open-air pavilion behind us," Trent said. "It leads to a rental space and the other section of the park."

"I'm aware of it." Audrey had been inside once for a high-school dance, years ago.

"The two of you head that way."

"And you?" she demanded.

"I'll be the distraction. Draw them to the pavilion."

"Dad, no."

Hunched over because of the cramped space, he cupped her cheek. "This is the only way."

She shook her head. "Julian, please. Think of another plan."

His eyes were dark with apology. "Divide and conquer. It's the best option we've got."

The space beneath the platform grew dimmer as the sun dipped lower. Time wasn't on their side. By now, the police had likely been notified of the disturbance and were on their way.

She took hold of Trent's hand and kissed it. "I love you, Dad."

"Stop worrying about me, young lady," he said gruffly. "Tan?"

"I'll guard her with my life."

He nodded a silent thank-you and, gun at his side, darted into the open.

Her heart in her throat, Audrey followed Julian out the opposite way. They made for the trees. Gunfire didn't immediately affect their progress, but she didn't dare glance back. Running along the copse edge, they reached the wide, wooden footbridge spanning the stream.

The *pop-pop-pop* riding on the breeze halted her in her tracks.

She spun around. Her dad was almost to the pavilion.

She watched him stumble and fall to the ground.

He didn't get up.

She willed him to get up.

He was lying there, unmoving. Vulnerable.

A man in a suit advanced at a rapid clip. If the first hit hadn't ended his life, the next one would. Gerald's goon would make sure of it.

She started forward. Julian's rock-solid grip locked onto her arms.

"Let go! We have to help him!"

"We've got trouble, Audrey."

He jerked his chin at the man striding in their direction. Gerald.

She looked back at her father. The gun-for-hire stood over his prone form and aimed for his head.

TWENTY-ONE

It was the helo catastrophe all over again.

Helplessness choked him. He couldn't reach Gunny in time. He was too far away to get off a clean shot, and Gerald was bearing down on them.

Julian had promised his superior he'd guard Audrey. She had to be his priority.

"We can't stay," he told her, urging her to move. Nothing good would come from her watching her father's demise. He knew from experience how those last moments stuck with a person, available for infinite replay.

But she refused to budge. Grief and horror were stamped onto her paper-white features.

He couldn't help another glimpse at the pavilion. He braced himself for the final shot.

It never came.

Gunny's motionless body erupted into action. He kicked the gun from the goon's hands.

A gasp of stunned disbelief vibrated through Audrey.

Surprise worked to Gunny's advantage. He planted another foot into the goon's sternum, knocking him backward. Gunny barreled into him.

They would've stood there, transfixed, if not for the bullet that dug into the railing near Audrey's hand.

This time, Julian didn't give her an opportunity to resist. He wrapped his arms around her waist and physically turned her toward their destination—a square building with far too many ceiling-to-floor windows and isolated on a manmade island in the midst of a lake.

One way in. One way out.

As soon as Audrey's feet met the ground, she sprinted along the bridge. Julian kept pace.

Not surprised to find the door locked, he kicked at the standard, cheap handle and splintered the wood frame. At his urging, Audrey wedged inside first. He hadn't expected the space to be littered with storage.

Without a word, he started scooting artificial Christmas trees in front of the door to obstruct Gerald's progress—if he chose to enter after them. If it had been Julian, he would find another way inside in order to avoid an ambush.

"What now?" Audrey demanded, shoving boxes in between the trees.

The shadows were deepening inside the building. "There are too many windows," he muttered, shaking his head. "But at least he won't have a clear view."

"We're almost completely surrounded by water," she added, grimacing. "It's not as deep or treacherous as the ocean, though."

They maneuvered between stacks of plastic bins and folding chairs. He listened for foreign sounds that would clue him into Gerald's whereabouts.

He pointed at the doors flanking the stage. "What's behind those?"

"I think one leads to the kitchen and prep area. And I recall bathrooms being back there." She twisted around. "Where's Gerald?"

"Probably looking for a different entrance."

"Should we exit the way we came?"

A distinctive, familiar sound registered, followed by splintering glass. "Get down!"

Julian dragged Audrey to the parquet floor and told her to crawl to the closest door and get herself through it. He skidded behind a plastic bin and returned fire.

"Julian," she called, waving him over. "Hurry!"

Still under attack, he dashed to where she waited, then snaked his arm around her waist and pulled her into the hallway. Or what he'd thought was a hallway.

"It's a dead end."

The three walls surrounding them offered scant options.

Window on their right. Sheetrock ahead. Bathroom on their left.

"Watch out!" she cried.

The window shattered, spewing glass shards at them. Audrey pushed open the bathroom door. They hurried inside for what would be a brief reprieve.

They were trapped.

"That wasn't Gerald, was it?" she said. "It was one of the twins."

He didn't have a chance to respond. The door swung open. He squeezed Audrey into the largest stall and, sending up a plea for help, pulled the trigger. Nothing happened. Out of ammo.

The hulking man smirked and prepared to unload in Julian's chest.

Julian wasn't ready to die. He had too much life to live. Life with Audrey, if she'd have him.

A perfectly placed jab in the neck stunned Sergei long enough for Julian to strike a second time, sending his weapon clattering to the floor. He belted his cheek with his pistol butt. The big man turned purple and charged. Julian twisted on his heel at the last possible second and helped his forward motion along, slamming him into the wall.

Dazed, Sergei sank onto the floor and clutched his head.

Sirens raged in the distance. As much as he dreaded the inevitable confrontation with law enforcement, he welcomed the assistance.

"Julian, look." Audrey had discovered a curtain in the

stall, the same color as the wall paint, that hid a door. She opened it. "A closet? There's another door leading somewhere. The stage or kitchen, maybe."

Approaching footsteps outside the bathroom spurred him on. They entered the storage room and closed and locked the door behind them. Audrey turned around, bumped into something and screamed.

He placed his hands on her shoulders and pulled her back against him, impatient for his eyes to adjust to the darkness. "What's wrong?"

"That." Shuddering, she poked at a tall silhouette. "Why would they store a mannequin in here?"

The knob rattled behind them. Skirting around the life-size mannequin, they navigated the tight space and emerged onto the stage.

"Sergei, I see them!"

Julian grabbed her hand again and made for the kitchen door this time. The hallway wasn't a dead end like the other one. He burst into the room first, only to skid to a stop.

Gerald was waiting for them.

"Sergeant Tan. Miss Harris. Time to join your friend Chasity."

There was no chance to react. No chance to block Audrey.

He shot her right in front of him.

Her lips parted, and her eyes locked onto Julian. Shock and regret swirled in the blue depths. She grabbed onto the counter but couldn't hold on.

Julian's vision blinked in and out. He launched himself over the island and rammed his feet into Gerald's chest. Within seconds, he had the older man beneath him on the ground, disarmed and at the mercy of his fists.

He didn't register the motion around him. Didn't care if the twins were about to end him.

The woman he loved would be avenged.

* * *

Audrey called Julian's name. Her voice sounded weak to her ears.

He didn't hear her. Police officers spilled into the industrial kitchen and separated him from Gerald. They kneeled beside her and instructed her to remain still until help arrived.

She tried to sit up. "I'm okay."

"You'll have to be checked out by a medical professional, ma'am."

An officer shifted, granting her a better glimpse of him. Blood dripped down his arm from the wound he'd suffered earlier. He was in handcuffs.

The sight sickened her. "He's innocent."

His head whipped in her direction, and his gaze, hazy with fury, sharpened and cleared. His jaw lost its lethal rigidity. His mouth softened.

"Audrey—" He strained toward her.

Still on the floor, she used her waning energy to reach out to him. But he was escorted through the open door and out into the night.

Pain belatedly speared her side. "He's done nothing wrong."

They didn't heed her words as they revived Gerald and, after brief questioning, took him outside.

The EMTs arrived then and loaded her onto a stretcher. She asked about her dad, but their lips were clamped tight. If she wasn't injured, she'd be in handcuffs, too.

The journey across the bridge was far from comfortable. With each jolt and bump, her nausea and pain increased. She couldn't see anything besides treetops and twinkling stars above due to the neck brace.

"Audrey!"

The EMTs slowed their pace as her dad jogged to her side. He looked as if he'd aged ten years in half an hour.

"Audrey, where are you hurt?"

"My side. It's not bad." She clung to his warm, calloused hand. Tears leaked from the corners of her eyes. "Are you okay?"

"Captain Brady returned in the nick of time. He saved me."

"We told him to stay away," she murmured. "Did you see Julian?"

His eyes became hooded. "He can handle himself."

"Dad—"

"We can't delay any longer." The men in charge of her care started forward again.

Trent walked faster. "I'll follow you to the hospital."

"Don't let them release Gerald," she called. "Tell them everything."

At the hospital, Audrey's wound was assessed and treated. She was fortunate, the ER doctor told her, that surgery wasn't required. The bullet went straight through and didn't do damage.

A pair of detectives grilled her for what seemed like hours until her father—his patience exhausted—intruded on their interrogation. They informed her they weren't arresting her, but she was required to stay in town until they said otherwise.

"Did you bring me a change of clothes?" She peeled off the hospital-issue blanket and searched for her shoes.

Trent stared at her in consternation. "Where do you think you're going? You haven't been discharged."

"Dad, Julian's in danger. Remember we told you about Officer Craddock?"

"Sergeant Tan has been transferred to Camp Lejeune. He's in military-police custody. Gerald and his cohorts are being interrogated at the Jacksonville police station."

"They won't mistreat him, will they? Do you think they tended his wound?"

"Audrey." His voice and face sharpened. "Your only concern should be your recovery."

His eyes were bloodshot, his jaw heavy with scruff— not a typical look for him. While she was impatient for answers, she understood what she'd put him through. Days of not knowing whether she was alive or dead. For much of her life, it had been dad and daughter against the world. He must've been out of his mind with heartache and worry.

She reached for him, and he took her hand. "I'm going to be fine, you know."

Blinking fast, he angled his face toward the window and cleared his throat. When he looked at her again, his eyes were moist. "I thank God for bringing you back to me."

"There were times I was sure we weren't going to make it out alive," she admitted. "But God delivered us." She took a deep breath. "I know you don't want to hear this, but I love Julian."

His stance lost some of its starch. "I was afraid you were going to say that."

"Do you have any objections to him as a person? Or is it simply the fact he's a marine?"

"He's a fine marine," he hedged.

"He's a decorated hero," she amended. "More than that, he's a *good* man. Julian's noble. Brave. Thoughtful and supportive. He's movie-star handsome—"

"You've made your point," he drawled. "I worried you wouldn't risk your heart again after Seth. You were alone for a very long time. But couldn't you have fallen for a civilian?"

"He's the one for me, Dad. I have to see him." She had to tell him what was in her heart, even if he didn't recip- rocate her feelings. "Will you take me to him?"

Trent reluctantly agreed. On the way to the base, he told her he'd seen Chasity.

The detectives had deigned to answer her questions about her friend. Gerald had made them think she'd died. She had actually survived the accident, but her prognosis was dire.

"It's bad, isn't it?"

"She's in a coma."

If she ever came out of it, she'd spend the rest of her life in prison. A tragedy and a waste. "It's difficult for me to fathom how she could've gotten caught up in something so terrible. She had a bright future, and now she's stuck in a hospital bed attached to tubes and machines." A fresh wave of grief washed over her. "Have you heard anything about Lincoln?"

"He's in custody, trading valuable information for promised leniency."

"He'll still spend a good chunk of his life in prison."

"Yes."

"And Officer Craddock?"

Trent scowled. "Brady turned Craddock's phone over to the department. I haven't heard anything more."

"Brady won't be charged for aiding us, I hope."

The captain was waiting for them outside PMO headquarters. He rushed to assist her out of the car. "You're looking peaked," he exclaimed. "You shouldn't have left the hospital."

Audrey dismissed his concern with a wave of her hand. She was weak, granted, and sore, but there was no reason to lounge in bed and be poked and prodded unnecessarily. "Have you seen him?"

Brady's expression solemn, he placed his arm gently around her shoulders and turned her toward the door. "He's somewhere in the building. That's all I know."

"What about you? Are you okay?"

"I'm not going to be disciplined for helping my friends, if that's what you're thinking."

After everything that had happened, Audrey considered Brady a friend, as well. She couldn't express how much his selfless support meant to her.

A cold breeze tousled her unbound hair. "Go inside before you get pneumonia," Trent said.

"You aren't coming?"

He cupped her upper arms and smiled down at her. "You and Sergeant Tan have things to sort out. Once that's done, I'll have a word with him."

"Dad—"

"I'm allowed to tell him to take care of my daughter, aren't I?"

"He may not feel the same way I do."

"Impossible."

Brady flashed a rare grin. "I have to concur with Gunny Harris. Julian is mad about you. Anyone with eyes can see that."

Audrey entered the waiting area first, approached the reception desk and set about getting answers. The young marine behind the counter was polite but evasive. Frustration mounted. She wanted—no, needed—to see for herself that Julian was all right.

She didn't see the side door open, but she heard the commotion—camera flashes and questions hurled by a military newspaper reporter.

Holding her breath, she turned and saw him surrounded by other marines.

Her heart swelled with gratitude. He was fine. Dirty and dusty, his brown-black hair mussed, he looked worn out but unharmed. No handcuffs in sight.

"Julian."

At the sound of her voice, he pushed forward, strode across the room and hauled her into his arms.

Julian could hardly contain his joy at being in her presence. He'd ached to see her, talk to her, hold her.

Remembering her injury, he released her. She was too pale for his liking. "You should be at the hospital."

"I had to see you. I was worried."

He gently smoothed a lock of her hair behind her ear. "I'm not the one who got shot at close range. Are you in pain?"

"Not with the medication they gave me." She inspected the fresh bandage around his biceps. "I'm happy to see they treated your arm."

The camera snapped again, reminding him they had an audience. He sought out Brady, who understood what he was trying to communicate. His friend strode to the reception desk, spoke to the marine and then ushered them through another door and into a private office. When they were alone, Audrey ignored his suggestion to sit. Instead, she wrapped her arms around his waist and rested her head against his chest.

"Is it really over?"

He returned her embrace and, smoothing her hair, kissed the crown of her head. "There will be more questions, but our names will be cleared and our reputations restored."

Thank You, Lord Jesus, for Your protection and deliverance from this fiery trial.

"The danger has passed?"

"I was told Lincoln is singing like a canary. The names of the dirty cops have been collected. Gerald and the twins are behind bars. Josef is dead. He didn't survive the crash. And the warehouse is being raided as we speak."

A tiny shudder worked through her. She lifted her head

and gazed up at him. "So this is an appropriate time to tell you that being friendly neighbors isn't enough anymore?"

His heart kicked against his ribs. He soaked in her features. She was so beautiful, so dear to him. "What are you saying, Audrey?"

"I don't want to go back to the way things were. I want to be with you. Do normal things like watch movies or go to restaurants. No exotic animals and no guns."

He caressed her silken cheek. "Our instructors preached the importance of not crossing personal lines in a protective duty assignment. I crossed them all, every single one."

Her brow wrinkled. "Do you regret it?"

"What?" He sucked in a harsh breath. "No, not at all. How could I? I fell in love with you, Audrey."

A tender smile brightened her features. "My honorable warrior." She framed his face and tipped up her mouth to his. "Oh, how I love you."

Julian hadn't known the power of those words when spoken by a woman he both admired and adored. A sense of belonging, of partnership and true, lasting connection filled him with confidence. He would no longer live in fear of failure or according to other peoples' expectations. He'd live for love and family, the one he hoped to build with Audrey.

She kissed him then, and the worry and stress of the last few weeks evaporated.

Audrey loved him. Nothing else mattered.

EPILOGUE

Four months later

"What are we doing here?" Audrey turned to the young woman behind the wheel. "I thought you wanted to go to the mall."

One of Julian's sisters, Melanie, shrugged and opened the driver's side door of her rental. "You don't like this restaurant?"

Through the windshield, she considered the stucco building and the shimmering water beyond the dock.

"It's actually a favorite of mine." Closing her door, she had to hurry to catch up to the black-haired beauty. "Did Julian recommend it?"

"He mentioned it once." Slowing, she hooked her arm through Audrey's and beamed at her. "I hope you don't mind the detour."

"I'd rather eat here than the food court, anyway."

"Good."

"I'm glad you came for a visit," Audrey told her. "I wish you could stay longer, though."

Melanie had arrived almost two weeks ago. Audrey's initial nervousness about meeting one of Julian's sisters had quickly dissipated. She was outgoing and genuine, and they shared a love of bookstores, cooking shows and shoes.

"I'm counting on seeing you again soon." Smiling, she nudged her shoulder.

Before she could ask about her future travel plans,

they reached the entrance to the deck where guests could enjoy outdoor seating. Every table was vacant except the last one, which was tucked in the far corner and framed by hot pink azalea bushes.

Her steps slowed. "What is this?"

Melanie slipped her arm free. "Go and see."

Julian, who'd been gazing at the cotton-candy sky above navy blue water, turned from the railing and straightened to his full height. He was dressed in crisp black dress pants and a gorgeous Hawaiian-style short-sleeve button-down. His dark hair was trimmed, the thatch on top short and spiky. He got more handsome every time she saw him.

Wearing a smile she'd come to crave, he approached and placed a fragrant lei around her neck. *"Aloha."*

"I thought you and Brady had a basketball game tonight."

He brushed a kiss on her cheek and settled an arm about her waist. "That was what I wanted you to think."

"Is this for my birthday?"

That wasn't for two more weeks, but maybe he'd chosen to celebrate early in order to surprise her. She was learning he liked to do that.

"Are you hungry?" he said, avoiding the question and leading her to a table straight out of an island fairy tale. White lights shimmered in glass containers. Pineapple shells contained vibrant blooms. Thick wooden platters sat atop green banana leaves.

"I had an early lunch, so yes, I'm famished."

He poured bright liquid into a goblet and handed it to her. "This is POG juice, a blend of passion fruit, orange and guava. A staple in the islands."

The taste was sweet and light. "I'm a fan."

He chuckled. "I've asked the chef to prepare a couple

of popular island dishes. The first is *pipikaula*, strips of dried and salted beef."

Audrey indulged in several bites before remembering Melanie. She searched the deck and area beyond. "I didn't notice Melanie leaving. And where are the other customers?"

"I reserved this space for us."

"You did? Impressive."

"Wait until you see what we have for dessert."

"What is it?"

He pulled out her chair and, once she was comfortable, sat opposite her.

"You'll have to wait and see."

His smile held a touch of mischief and his eyes sparkled. Contentment settled deep inside, along with overwhelming gratitude. She thanked God for blessing her with this man.

A young man served them one dish after another. The meal was sumptuous and unique. When he brought out the chocolate macadamia ice cream pie, she savored every bite.

Julian grinned.

"I could eat this every day."

He put down his fork and sank against his chair. "You like island fare?"

"What's not to like?"

"I'm glad to hear you say that." Reaching for a thick envelope tucked in between the flower arrangements, he handed it to her.

There was no writing on it. She couldn't imagine what it might be.

"Open it," he urged, the easy humor gone from his face.

Audrey did as he'd instructed and stared at the boarding passes. "This is too much, Julian."

His expression earnest, he said, "I want you to see my home, to experience it with me. I also want the rest of my family to meet you."

Her heart did the hula. "This is the best birthday present," she gushed, jumping up to hug him. "And this…" Straightening, she swept her arm to encompass the table and perfect view. "This is a memory I'll treasure."

"The tickets aren't for your birthday."

"They aren't?"

He left his chair, took her hand and went down on one knee. "Audrey, you taught me the meaning of true courage. You showed me what loving selflessly and without reservation looks like."

She lifted her trembling hand to her mouth. "Oh, Julian."

His eyes brimmed with pride and joy. "I love you. I want to spend the rest of my life with you. Will you marry me?"

"I will," she said through a smile and tears. "I love you, too."

He produced an elegant, round-cut diamond ring and slid it onto her finger. Then he pulled her into his arms and delivered a toe-curling kiss that stole her breath away. When he lifted his head, he caressed her cheek.

"We could have an island ceremony, if that's what you want."

The thought of her and Julian exchanging vows amid sweeping seas and lush, island scenery pleased her immensely. "That sounds like a dream wedding."

"We can take some time to decide," he said, lacing his hands behind her back. "I had the meeting with my doc today."

She gasped. "That was supposed to have been next week, right? What did he say?"

"He gave me the option of joining a new team or being an instructor."

Ecstatic he wasn't going to be forced to retire, she searched his face for clues. "And?"

"The more I think about it, the more inclined I am to be an instructor. I'd be able to pass what I've learned on to new guys."

"You'll be a source of wisdom and inspiration for them. I'm proud of you."

"You ready to be a marine wife?"

She kissed him. "Does that answer your question?"

"I can't wait to start our life together."

She smiled up at him. "Didn't you know? We already have."

* * * * *

If you enjoyed this book,
look for the first book in this series
Explosive Reunion.

Dear Reader,

Thank you for choosing to read this second book about US Marine Corps heroes. There's a saying among authors that some books seem to write themselves. This happened to be one of them. From the beginning, Julian and Audrey proved to be fun, interesting characters to explore. I liked the idea of passing acquaintances whose paths might not ever cross, if not for extraordinary circumstances. I hope you enjoyed their story. Next up is Captain Brady Johnson.

Find more about my books at www.karenkirst.com. I'm also on Facebook and Twitter, @KarenKirst. You can also email me at karenkirst@live.com.

Blessings,
Karen Kirst

COMING NEXT MONTH FROM
Love Inspired® Suspense

Available September 3, 2019

TRAIL OF DANGER
True Blue K-9 Unit • by Valerie Hansen

When Abigail Jones wakes up injured from an attack she doesn't remember, she knows someone's after her, but she doesn't know *why*. Now only the man who rescued her, Officer Reed Branson, and his K-9 partner can keep her safe while she regains her memory.

DANGEROUS RELATIONS
The Baby Protectors • by Carol J. Post

When her sister is killed, Shelby Adair's determined to keep her young niece away from the father's shady family—especially since she's convinced they were behind the murder. But after the killer attempts to kidnap little Chloe, can Shelby trust the child's uncle, Ryan McConnell, with their lives?

DEADLY EVIDENCE
Mount Shasta Secrets • by Elizabeth Goddard

FBI agent Tori Peterson intends to find her sister's murderer, even if it makes her a target. But that means returning home and working with the lead detective—her ex-boyfriend, Ryan Bradley. With someone willing to kill to keep the truth hidden, can Tori and Ryan survive the investigation?

UNDERCOVER TWIN
Twins Separated at Birth • by Heather Woodhaven

Audrey Clark never knew she was a twin—until she stumbled onto a covert operation. Now with her FBI agent sister in critical condition, Audrey's the only one who can complete the mission. But with danger around every corner, can she avoid falling for her pretend husband, FBI agent Lee Benson?

RECOVERED SECRETS
by Jessica R. Patch

Two years ago, a woman with amnesia washed up on the banks of search-and-rescue director Hollis Montgomery's small Mississippi town. The woman he calls Grace still has no idea who she really is, but they finally have a clue: someone wants her dead.

FATAL MEMORIES
by Tanya Stowe

It's DEA agent Dylan Murphy's job to take down a drug ring, including border patrol officer Jocelyn Walker's brother. But he's not sure whether Jocelyn is innocent...and without her memory, neither is she. Now it's Dylan's job to protect her from the gang dead set on silencing her for good.

LISCNM0819

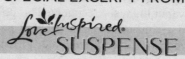
Abigail Jones stared at the blackening eastern sky and shivered. She was more afraid of the strangers lingering in the shadows along the Coney Island boardwalk than she was of the summer storm brewing over the Atlantic.

Early September humidity made the salty oceanic atmosphere feel sticky while the wind whipped loose tendrils of Abigail's long red hair. If sixteen-year-old Kiera Underhill hadn't insisted where and when their secret meeting must take place, Abigail would have stopped to speak with some of the other teens she was passing. Instead, she made a beeline for the spot where their favorite little hot dog wagon spent its days.

Besides the groups of partying youth, she skirted dog walkers, couples strolling hand in hand and an old woman leaning on a cane. Then there was a tall man and enormous dog ambling toward her. As they passed beneath an overhead vapor light, she recognized his police uniform and breathed a sigh of relief. Most K-9 patrols in her nearby neighborhood used German shepherds, so seeing the long floppy ears and droopy jowls of a bloodhound brought a smile despite her uneasiness.

Pausing, Abigail rested her back against the fence surrounding a currently closed amusement park, faced into the wind and waited for the K-9 cop to go by. His unexpected presence could be what was delaying Kiera.

"Come on, Kiera. I came alone, just like you wanted," Abigail muttered.

Kiera had sounded panicky when she'd phoned.

"Here. Over here" drifted on the wind. Abigail strained to listen.

The summons seemed to be coming from inside the Luna Park perimeter fence. That was not good since the amusement facility was currently closed. Nevertheless, she cupped her hands around her eyes and peered through the chain-link fence. It was several seconds before she realized the gate was ajar. *Uh-oh. Bad sign.* "Kiera? Is that you?"

A disembodied voice answered faintly. "Help me! Hurry."

Don't miss
Trail of Danger *by Valerie Hansen,*
available September 2019 wherever
Love Inspired® Suspense books and ebooks are sold.

www.LoveInspired.com

LISEXP0819